# STOLEN FROM A DREAM

## NIRANJAN

Editing by Fair Editions
Cover Design by Wynter Designs
Formatted by Fair Editions

# DEDICATION

TO MY HUSBAND

HAPPY BIRTHDAY

I LOVE YOU

# THIS BOOK CONTAINS THE FOLLOWING CONTENT AND TRIGGER WARNINGS

1. DEATH, MURDER
2. POISON, BLOOD, VIOLENCE
3. DOMESTIC ABUSE
4. GRIEF, LOSS, PAIN
5. CHILDBIRTH, PREGNANCY
6. ALCOHOL CONSUMPTION
7. DEATH OF A FAMILY MEMBER
8. BETRAYAL
9. MIND CONTROL
10. GASLIGHTING
11. DROWNING
12. TRAUMA, PTSD

# Stolen From A Dream

# PROLOGUE

"We have to go!" Her father sounded tense and Leithia looked at him from where she was playing with her doll. He was dressed in black clothes and had a hood on. A bag was strapped to his back.

"Darien?" Leithia's mother asked, rising from where she sat, sewing a tear in one of Leithia's dresses. She placed a hand on her full belly. "What happened?"

"No time to explain, Seania," Father said, holding out a black cloak with a hood. "We have to leave now!"

Leithia looked at the window through which could be seen the heavy rain falling outside.

"Father, it's raining," she said. "We'll get wet."

"It's all right, Leithia," her mother said, turning to her. "Get up and come; see, we all have matching cloaks."

The black cloak was warm, and smelled faintly of spices. The hood fell down almost to her eyes. Leithia took her mother's hand, and they followed their father outside. There was a small wagon outside with a cover, and Father helped Mother and Leithia up before climbing on to the driver's seat.

"There are no horses," Leithia whispered to her mother.

"Hush, Leithia," her mother said, holding her close to her breast. "Stay quiet for a bit, please, my darling, and don't look outside."

There were shouts and screams coming from somewhere, and the wagon started moving. Leithia wanted to ask her mother what was happening, but she dared not. Her mother had asked her to be quiet, which was something her mother had never asked her before.

It was so hard, however, and Leithia started humming one of the lullabies her mother used to sing, but her voice was lost in the sound of thunder from outside.

"Darien," her mother said, her voice sounding strange. "My water has broken."

"Hold on a moment longer, Seania," Father said and the wagon's speed increased for just a moment before it stopped, and everything was still.

Father climbed up onto the wagonbed. "Leithia," he said. "Your mother is going to give birth. Go, sit in front, and don't leave the wagon, understand? Don't talk to anyone you might see and don't make any sounds."

Leithia nodded, though she didn't understand what was going on. "I want to see the baby," she said.

"You will see the baby when it's born," Father said. "Now, go sit in the front, and don't move and don't make any sounds."

Leithia's eyes widened and her mouth fell open as she went to the front. There was nothing but white sand wherever she looked. No trees, no grass, nothing. Their wagon was standing on a narrow road paved with black bricks. The sky was red and there was no sun or moon. No clouds either.

Leithia's heart beat fast as she saw someone appear suddenly to her right. They were wearing a hood like the one Father had, but there was something about the way they moved that made Leithia press back against the seat, her hand over her mouth to stifle her frightened whimper.

They stopped when they were almost at the wagon, lifted their head and sniffed the air.

"Blood," they said, except it echoed eerily, as if it came from somewhere very deep, reminding Leithia of how it sounded when she shouted into the unused old well back in her village.

Three more people appeared, all identical to the first one. Leithia couldn't see any of their faces.

"What is it, Basor?" one of them asked.

"Blood," Basor replied. "Human blood is here."

"Nonsense," another one scoffed. "No human can come here. This is our kingdom."

"Nevertheless, a human is here, and I smell their blood."

"We have more important things to worry about," the third one interrupted. "The Gods have found our door. We need to make sure they won't be able to open it."

All four vanished, but Leithia stayed where she was, unmoving, her hand still in her mouth.

The wail of a baby broke the silence but stopped almost immediately, as if it was smothered by something. Leithia glanced behind her, wishing she could go inside.

"Leithia," her father called softly. "Come here and meet your brother."

Leithia scrambled to the back and saw the tiny baby suckling at her mother's breast. He looked wrinkled and ugly, and she frowned.

"Why is he so small?" she asked.

"All babies are small," her father said. He leaned over to kiss the top of Mother's head. "We should get going. We can't stay long."

The wagon started moving again. Her mother held the little bundle that held Leithia's little brother close to her chest. Leithia sat next to her, looking at the baby.

"What's his name?" she whispered.

"Pelthiel," her mother murmured. She looked pale, and there were streaks of blood on her hair and hands.

Before Leithia could ask something about that, there was a crash of lightning, and everything went dark. The wagon suddenly picked up speed, and Leithia held on to her mother, shutting her eyes tight.

The wagon stopped without a jolt.

"Dariel?" her mother asked, and Leithia opened her eyes. It was still dark, and it seemed to be raining, drops falling heavily on the wagon's top, the sound loud.

"We're here," her father said. "But they're coming, and I need to draw them off."

"No!" Her mother sounded frightened. "You're not strong enough! Don't do this, Dariel!"

"I have no choice," he said quietly. "Take the children, Seania. Keep them safe. Make sure they won't find them or you."

"Dariel!"

"Warn them when they're old enough," Father said, as though he couldn't hear Mother. "They should know, and they should be careful."

He climbed on the back, water running down his hood, which he pushed back. He looked strange, pale, and Leithia didn't know what was happening.

"Father," she whispered.

"Leithia, my darling." Her father touched her cheek, and he swallowed, his eyes filling. "I love you more than anything. I hope you know that."

His hand moved to the head of the baby. "Pelthiel... I wish I could have known you more, but I love you already."

He leaned to kiss Mother, and drew back, his forehead against hers, and Mother was crying, tears flowing down her cheeks.

"You're the best thing that ever happened to me, Seania, and it was my good fortune that you chose to love me, despite all the dangers it brought. All I ask... all I want is that you should hold on a while longer, my love. Remember that I love you... and I will do everything I can to protect you."

"I love you," Mother whispered. "I'll always love you, Dariel. No matter what happens, I will love you."

"Protect our children," Father whispered.

"With my life," Mother answered. "As you're doing now."

Father kissed her once more. "The wagon will take you to our new home." He turned to Leithia and kissed her cheeks and forehead. "I love you," he said. "Be good to your brother, okay? He's tiny and will need help till he grows. Mother will tell you stories and make you dolls."

"Father," she sobbed, not knowing what was happening, but her heart felt like it will burst with how her chest squeezed. "Don't leave."

Because she could tell that he was going to.

"I wish I could stay," he said. "Oh, darling, I wish it more than anything... but I have to go, Leithia. I love you."

He went out the back, and all Leithia saw before the flap closed was a dark yawning mouth and lightning all around it.

# ONE

The ocean had always seemed like a friend to Pel. As he waded in to gather shells for his sister to make the trinkets that she would later infuse with magic and sell at the market, he felt its affection like a warm blanket enveloping him.

Serityl, she sang her name to him, a name that was not familiar to him. His mother had never told him anything about the ocean or about why it seemed like a friend.

But then, his mother hadn't told them anything much, the sickness that took her coming so suddenly and ending her so swiftly. All she managed to do with her last breath was adjure them both to beware the Gods.

Pel wished he knew why. It wasn't that he was eager to meet any of the Gods, but why had his mother warned them both against them?

He looked at the ocean, so vast, so blue. What lay at the other end of it? Would he ever find out? The island they lived in was small, off the coast of the mainland of Hevad. They had been to the large market on the mainland a few times, but that was the extent of their travels.

What would it be like to cross this ocean, to see what lay at the other end of it? What lay there? Would there be lands where people looked the same, dressed the same, spoke the same language? In the great fair at the mainland, there had been stories of people from other lands with skin as pale as snow and hair of different colours.

Pel didn't know that he trusted those stories. Most of the stories claimed the Gods to be good, but their mother had told them to be careful of them, and he trusted his mother.

The Gods of Beltoros weren't a nice lot if you looked beneath the stories, for all the sweeping statements of their goodness that were made by the storytellers. The Gods always seemed too vindictive to Pel, punishing even the smallest infractions more than was warranted, and even to those who followed them faithfully, no rewards were given. More than that, the Gods seemed susceptible to bribery and flattery themselves.

If they were good, no one would fear them, and many of the Gods were feared more than loved. Utfer, especially, with the city of Nagir still practising human sacrifice, and even the King powerless to stop it because what king can stand against a God?

Pel sighed. It was none of his business what the people of Nagir did. The city was far away, even if they went to the mainland. It was nominally part of the kingdom, but no garrison was stationed there, and they paid no tribute, it was said. Not that Pel knew. All his information came from gossip overheard while they were on the mainland.

He picked a few more shells, wishing he had Leithia's gifts of imbuing objects with magic. He could have helped her more. All he could do was—what exactly? Create fire? Cause storms? Not serious ones, but small ones. His magic was battle magic, they had learned, and it might help if they ever had to fight anyone. In a war.

Except Pel didn't want to be a soldier. He wanted to be a scholar, and to study, and read. He already had a collection of books and scrolls that he was proud of. Any extra coin they had went towards books, which was something he and his sister had in common. While she had no aspirations towards scholarship, Leithia was as well read as Pel and as enamoured of books.

Pel had once asked his sister what she wanted to be, and she had looked at the ocean, a look of longing in her eyes. "To sail in these waters," she said. "To explore, to discover unknown places."

Leithia had no gifts to control the weather, and even Pel was not too good at it. Without that, the only way to travel would be to pay, and Pel knew that neither of them could afford it.

Not yet, anyway.

"Someday," he had told her, holding her close. "Someday we will save enough money to sail around the world."

She had laughed. "And what will you do?" she teased him. "Stay locked in your cabin all day reading something? You can do that here with far less damage to your eyes and our finances."

"Well, if you don't want me to come with you, you just have to say it," Pel had said with mock sorrow.

Leithia had punched him.

Pel had, without telling Leithia, started saving since, however. They made so very little from their fishing and crops and selling the trinkets that Leithia made, that it wasn't much, but Pel was hopeful. There was a fair coming up on the mainland, and they always made a lot during those.

"Pel," Leithia was coming towards him, her dress hitched up, and the water lapping at her knees. "It's getting late."

"There's still light," he said. "It's not as if we will drown, anyway."

The ocean wouldn't hurt them. It was something he knew in his bones.

"Still," she said. "Supper will get cold. I made your favourite stew."

Pel flushed guiltily. "It was my turn to cook," he said repentantly.

"I know," she smiled at him. "It's okay. I would have waited for you, but I needed something to do today."

Leithia got restless at times, and such occasions always preceded a vision.

"Let's go home," he said, putting the shells inside the bag hung from his belt. "If a vision's coming, it's better to be in the house."

Leithia grimaced. "I hate some of those," she said.

Pel couldn't blame her.

# TWO

L eithia loved dawns. When the sun was just breaking through the horizon, and the sky took on every hue of reds and oranges and pinks, and everything was quiet, except for the waves, was her favourite time of the day. Today was no different. Despite how she felt, the restlessness that often took her portending a vision, she was glad to be up early, and to sit on the rocks outside their small hut, making a bracelet. It will have a small protection charm, and another spell for luck. Both spells would last at least five years. It was the least expensive of the trinkets she made, but the one most in demand.

She looked across at the breaking dawn and remembered watching her mother make such trinkets. Leithia didn't have her mother's skill, though she was much better than Pel. Pel was all thumbs when it came to making anything, but he was good at repairs, and collecting things, and cooking.

Leithia looked towards the house where Pel was likely still asleep. She couldn't help but feel protective of him. Five years separated them, but it was more than that. She remembered the baby her father had put in her arms and told her to be good to him.

Not that it had ever been a hardship for her.

Leithia was not a fool, and she had always been better read than most people of her station. Her mother had taught both of them to read and write, and in doing so, had handed Leithia the key to unlocking the mystery of her father's last words and actions.

She had been five, but that day was branded into her memory. She had asked her mother, but she had always said *wait, I'll tell you when you're older,* and then she had taken ill and died and all she said was to *beware the Gods.*

To be fair, that was the most important clue.

Leithia looked at the ocean. Serityl, who sang her to sleep in the days and nights following her mother's death, who always gave the choicest of fish to her and Pel's nets, who brought the most beautiful shells and even an odd pearl or two to them.

Serityl, who talked to her of times long gone, of her family butchered by the Gods, of the spell that held her prisoner in the waters.

Leithia knew that she wasn't powerful enough to free her. She would never be. Her gifts were not in cursebreaking, but in crafting protections and luck.

And the unwanted gift of her visions.

Sometimes, Leithia felt like the doll she had left behind in her old house. Something that no one paid attention to when it came to it. Something expendable, to be discarded. She wondered if Pel felt the same way. Logically, she knew that her parents hadn't left them out of choice. Death was not a choice, after all. Even her father had chosen to stay behind so they would have the chance to get away safely.

A shudder passed through her, and she recognised it as

12

prelude to a vision. She leapt to her feet, dropping the shells and beads while she ran for the house. Being outside was often risky. Once inside, she closed the door and leaned against it. Not a moment later, she fell, down, down, down till she knew no more.

When she opened her eyes, she was on a boat in the ocean. The waters had never been this violent, waves rising above her head, as if intent on drowning her. Wind buffeted her boat and no matter how she tried, she couldn't control the craft.

She wanted to scream, tell Serityl it was her, but the words wouldn't come. She pulled at the tiller, and her arms were muscled, she saw, her hands larger and calloused. Her body felt heavier and strange.

Another wave crashed against her boat, and she cast her magic to keep the boat together even as she knew it was futile. This was Serityl's domain and her powers had no limits. Her own, on the other hand, had little effect. Leithia tried to scream again, but couldn't.

The next wave broke the boat apart, and Leithia fell into the ocean, reaching desperately for her magic, but found nothing. She tried to hang on to a log, but the water snaked around her ankles, pulling her down.

The song of the ocean was angry, vengeful, gloating, and it was a crescendo in her ears as she jerked up and screamed.

"Leithia!" Pel's frightened voice shook her out of her vision, and she stared blankly at her brother, and realisation crashed on her that she was in her house, safe.

"I'm fine," she whispered. The angry song of Serityl still reverberated in her ears and she tasted salt and copper on her tongue where she had bitten it so hard that it bled.

"A vision?" Pel asked, sitting in front of her, his hands on her shoulder, anchoring her, warming her. "Why didn't you wake me?"

"Wasn't enough time," she whispered, blinking back the tears from her eyes. "I hate this, Pel. I wish I didn't have it."

Pel held her, murmuring, "It's okay, Leit. I've got you."

She calmed down. "I was in the ocean," she said. "And there was a storm... I was going to drown and die..."

Pel looked outside, saying, "Looks like a storm is rolling in, Leit."

Leithia looked out the window and frowned. "Do you think he is out there? The man I saw?"

"Do you want to go look for him?" Pel asked.

Leithia bit her lip as she looked outside again. The ocean had never harmed them, and she knew it never would.

"Yes," she said, getting up. She grinned at him. "It could be fun, you know. We've never been in the ocean in a storm."

Pel sighed, but got up. "Your idea of fun is disturbing, my sister."

But he came with her, as she had known he would. All she hoped now was that they would get to the unknown man in her vision in time.

# THREE

The wave crashed into the boat, nearly overturning it, and Pelthiel swore under his breath. From the prow, Leithia laughed.

"This is fun, Pel!"

"To you, maybe!" he shouted. "I hope you'll still think it's fun when we've drowned."

"Don't be melodramatic!" she shouted back. "It's only a bit of water!"

That might be a matter of perspective. The waves rose higher than the cliffs where Pel had his home and the sky was grey. It was difficult to see anything due to the rain that was falling in torrents around them.

But the ocean had never harmed them, and Pel knew it wouldn't now either.

"I don't even know how we'll find them," he said. "It's a big ocean, Leit. They could be miles from where we are!"

The cold should have been numbing, but he had cast a small spell which was keeping him warm and dry. Leithia's spell was stronger, and it was keeping the boat upright and keeping them steady on their course, though Pel had no idea what it was.

"I told you, I have a feeling," she said. "They're around here, and they will drown if we don't help them. I just want something good to come out if my visions for once."

"Any fool who comes out in this weather deserves to drown," Pel muttered half-heartedly as another wave rose up, carrying their tiny boat on its crest.

"Hang on!" Leithia cried.

Pel didn't need to be told twice as he cast a quick spell that would make sure they wouldn't fall off when the wave crashed.

"Pel, we have magic," Leithia shouted as the wave began its descent at dizzying speed. "What's the point of being so powerful if we're not going to use it to help others?"

"Having magic doesn't make us all-powerful or immortal," Pel shouted, thankful for the howling wind and screaming waves that made his voice inaudible to his sharp eared sister.

For some reason, his thoughts went to a conversation he had overheard when he was little, when his mother had told Leithia that their father had liked helping people with his magic. She had fallen silent after that and had sighed. Pel had been too young to know what it meant, but now he wondered if their mother had been about to warn Leithia about using magic to help people.

Leithia didn't like talking about their father, though Pel knew she remembered him. Pel had never met him, and wasn't really certain what happened except that their father had died, and he had been trying to protect them.

Protect them from who, though? The Gods?

Their mother's last cryptic warning came to his mind, and

16

Pel shivered, though his spell still kept him warm.

The wave crashed down and if not for Leithia's spell, the boat would have splintered into fragments. Pel was nauseous from the sudden fall, and though he lost his footing and landed on his butt, he stayed inside the boat.

"Thanks," he said sourly to no one in particular.

Leithia laughed as she clung to the boat's prow, the waves and the wind buffeting her. She had not cast any spell to protect herself from the elements and was drenched to the skin, and was shivering violently.

"Is it your intention to die of cold?" he shouted as he did a quick spell to keep her dry and warm.

His reserves were almost exhausted. If they didn't find whoever they came to find, they were going to be in trouble. His warming spell was wearing off, and soon he would need to replenish that. He did a quick calculation in his head. He had enough stores left for three more small spells.

"Do you have any reserves in case it takes longer than we think?" he yelled.

"Don't worry!" Her voice floated back to him. "We'll be fine!"

Easy for her to say. It was sometimes difficult to believe she was the elder. It was Pel who had to be the voice of reason when Leithia got like this, who had to be more responsible. Leithia was not impulsive or reckless, but at times she became so, especially when it came to doing something to help others. Pel knew it all came from her large heart and trusting nature. It was up to him to hold her back and to keep her safe and make certain he had enough spells in reserve when they got into situations like this.

Had their father been like this? Had that got him into trouble with the Gods?

"There!" Leithia pointed, and half turned to him. "What did I tell you?"

Pel could see nothing, and he wasn't about to waste one of his precious spells in trying to see better. Instead, he stayed where he was, trusting his sister and her spell to take them towards whatever it was she saw. Soon, they came abreast with the object to which Leithia had pointed. It was a piece of wood floating in the water, probably broken off from some boat.

"Doesn't look like a person," Pel said.

She pointed again, and this time Pel saw it. A dark shape, bulky, bobbing in the water. If it was a person, they could already be dead.

*Please don't be dead!*

It was going to break Leithia's heart if they were too late.

"Help me, Pel," Leithia said as her spell pulled the floating person closer.

It was a man from what Pel could see, and they were clinging to a larger piece of wood. Had they been in a shipwreck? He hadn't asked Leithia for details of her vision. But it looked more like a boatwreck. Apart from the piece the man was clinging to and the smaller piece they had seen earlier, there was no other debris to be seen. He helped Leithia with the spell, and soon, the man, wet and shivering and unconscious, was on the bottom of their boat. But they weren't dead. Not yet.

"They're not going to last long if we don't get them to shore quickly," Pel said.

"I know," Leithia said, her face troubled.

The boat wasn't going to be fast enough to save him.

Pel sighed.

"I hate you so much," he said as he used the last of his spells and the last reserves of his warming spell on the boat, which turned around and shot like an arrow across the sea.

"Pel!" Leithia looked pale. "It's too strong for you!"

He was aware of it, the spell draining him faster than any other spell had, but he held on. Leithia would have been able to do it, had she any reserves left. She was stronger, more powerful. But she couldn't right now, because she had nothing left, and he did, so it was up to him to do it. It hurt, real, physical pain; the spell was ripping him apart and he could see his skin breaking, gashes appearing, and he gritted his teeth.

*I will not yield!*

A rush of something and he was feeling better, his skin was healing, and he was feeling more energised. The pain had subsided, and he felt clearheaded, his vision sharper. Land appeared in front of them, the cliffs looming before, majestic and implacable, and Leithia's direction spell guided their boat to the small cove from which they had started.

"Did you do something?" he asked as he looked at Leithia.

She shook her head, her eyes round with surprise as she looked at him.

"Pel," her voice was hushed, awed. "I think you just came into your power."

Pel felt his breath catch. He had only heard of it happening. Not everyone came into their powers. No one knew how it happened or why, but those who did were said to be able to command anything, any element, any object.

A wind swept over him, making him shiver, and Serityl sang in his ears, a song of victory.

Pel didn't feel victorious. He felt cold, and tired, and anxious.

19

# FOUR

eithia cleaned and dressed the stranger's injuries. They stayed unconscious, and she couldn't explain to herself the wariness she felt. There was something about the stranger that made her afraid. She was beginning to wish she had never tried to save them, though she couldn't explain why. They were injured from the boat breaking apart, and Pel's clothes were a perfect fit on them.

Pel was the one who had dried and dressed them in his clothes, though Leithia had rolled her eyes at him. He was not adept at healing, though, which was why this fell to her. She was too exhausted to cast any healing spells, however, and nothing seemed broken, so she just bound his wounds and left it at that.

She found her brother in the kitchen, stirring the stew.

"How is he?" Pel asked.

"I think he'll be fine," Leithia said. "We got all the water out of him, and his wounds are shallow. I'll heal them once I'm better. For now, I've cleaned and dressed them."

Pel gave one more stir before removing the stew from the stove, carrying it to their tiny table.

"Leit," he said. "What do you remember of our father?"

Leithia's heart hammered in her chest. She had avoided the subject of their father as much as she could, even though she knew she wouldn't be able to do it forever. Pel was not a child, and perhaps he should know.

Knowing could protect him, but she still felt reluctant, especially with the stranger a wall away.

"He was always cheerful," she said. "Good with his hands. There was nothing he couldn't make or mend... He used to make me dolls to play with, out of old bits of cloth and wood. He was... he was large, I think, though it might have been because I was small... he was... he loved us very much, Pel."

Pel was looking at his bowl of stew. "I wish I could have known him," he said.

"I wish the same," she whispered. "He... before he left, he said... he said that he already loved you, and wished that he could have got to know you, to see you grow up... He was a good man, Pel... he... I wish I knew why he had to go, why he had to die... I just... I wish a lot of things!"

"But you know something," he said. "Though you're not telling me."

Her brother had always been perceptive, and he had always known her better than she realised.

"What I know is... it's like what I suspect or theories rather than anything concrete, Pel... I don't even know if I should tell you."

"I want to know, Leit," Pel said. "I'm not a child anymore, and I... I want to know."

She had been afraid of this, she realised. She wished their mother was there so she could at least confirm what she suspected.

"I remember the day you were born," she said. "The day

21

our father died... he... we were escaping something, Pel... I don't know what, but he..." She remembered the empty sands, the hooded people, or creatures, her father adjuring her not to talk to anyone. A shudder went through her. "Let's... let's not talk of it now, please. Wait till the morning."

Pel's eyes held love and compassion. "Of course, Leit. I'm sorry that I brought up all the bad memories."

She shook her head. "Not like they ever leave," she said quietly. "And it isn't your fault, Pel. You have a right to know, even if it's only conjecture... at least if I'm wrong, you can tell me that."

They ate in silence. The stew was good, but Leithia tasted only ashes in her mouth. She had no idea why she felt like something was about to happen, something bad. It was not the same way she felt before her visions. This was a kind of bone deep caution and fear, and it was somehow associated with the stranger they had rescued.

"If we're to have food and medicines, I'll need to go to town tomorrow," she said. "Perhaps I could sell a few trinkets as well."

She hadn't made a lot, but hopefully the few she did and what remained of their savings would be enough.

Pel frowned. "I can go," he offered. "I have nothing to do here, and maybe I can find some work as well."

It was a good solution, but somehow the thought of being alone in the house with the stranger made Leithia's skin crawl.

"No, I... I need to get out of the house, Pel," she said. "I will tell you everything I know and suspect in the morning, and heal our guest before, though."

"Oh," Pel looked towards the room where the stranger lay. "I hope he survives. I wonder why the ocean was so violent. I've never seen it that way."

22

Leithia hadn't either. Usually, Serityl calmed when they were around. But earlier, it was as if she didn't care if they got hurt as long as she got the stranger to drown. Leithia supposed she could ask the ocean, but doubted she would get an answer. Serityl wasn't all there, whatever happened to bind her to the waters too horrific to her sanity and her mind.

After dinner, Pel lay down to sleep, but Leithia was too restless, so she made her way down to the beach.

"I'm afraid," she told Serityl. "He's asking questions, and I don't even know if I have any answers... I wish.. I wish you could tell me anything... I wish my mother were here... I wish Dad hadn't died... I just... it all feels so strange, Serityl. Why am I so afraid?"

The ocean made no answer, but she sounded joyful, just as she did when Pel's powers manifested. Leithia sighed. What had she been hoping for, anyway?

# FIVE

The morning came with no hint of the storm that had rocked the ocean the day before. Pel was up early, looking for his sister, and finding her outside. She looked troubled, but her fingers were steadily stringing together shells and beads. Pel went to her and sat by her, handing her the beads and shells in silence.

"You know that Serityl is sentient," Leithia said. "That she is bound to the waters. She is a powerful ancient being who controls all the waters, and once, she was free to go where she wanted, but then the Gods bound her to the oceans."

It was a folktale that they had heard once when they were on the mainland.

"I remember the story," Pel said. "It said that she grew arrogant in her power, so the Gods bound her to the waters."

Leithia snorted. "That's a bunch of nonsense," she said. "The true story... Serityl and her siblings lived in this world before the Gods came. They were powerful, with control over elements and other natural forces. Their magic was equal to that of the Gods. But the Gods saw in them a threat, and there was a great battle when the Gods managed to defeat Serityl and her siblings. In the end, Serityl and her siblings created a world for themselves, a dimension, if you will, and lived there." She sighed. "Till the Gods decided that they couldn't be allowed to live and went after them. They killed all of them except Serityl, who sought refuge in the ocean, and the Gods couldn't enter the waters because her power there was absolute. So they cast a spell to bind her to the ocean, and it drove her insane."

Pel frowned. "What has it to do with our father?"

"I think our father was one of them," she said, her voice very low. "That he... he came to this world to be with our mother, and that was how the Gods found them... he took us to safety and went to fight them and died, and that is why Mother warned us to beware of them."

Pel looked at the ocean, his heart suddenly squeezing tight. "You mean, we're not human."

"Not all human, anyway," she said. "And I... Pel, yesterday... that wasn't you coming to your power... it was always your power... it was only waiting... I... I think that you somehow inherited all their powers which means that you're more powerful than any God, and they... they will probably see you as a threat."

"Then we will stay here," Pel said. "Or at least, I will. No one will find me, Leit, or you. I will not even go to the mainland."

He didn't think it would be that simple, but he could hope.

Leithia put aside the trinkets she had made. "I'll heal our guest before I go," she said. "You should keep an eye on them, Pel. If it looks like he's getting worse, portal to me. I'll be in the market."

Pel nodded as he got up, picking up the basket from the

ground and following her inside.

He watched anxiously as Leithia healed the man they had brought. He couldn't explain why he felt so concerned, but he did. They had saved them, and Pel didn't think he could bear it if something happened to the man now.

Leithia left soon after, and Pel set about cleaning the house and preparing for lunch. In between, he watched the stranger whom they had saved. They hadn't gained consciousness yet, but Pel wasn't too worried about it. It wasn't to be expected that they would so soon. He and Leithia had changed them into dry clothes and had kept them warm, which was all they could do.

Pel remembered the man's body and felt his cheeks grow warm. The man had a perfect body, but Pel was supposed to be taking care of them, not drool over them. Pel couldn't determine their age. There were so many lines of pain on their face when they had brought them in, but now that face was smooth and peaceful. It was also an extremely attractive face with an ageless quality about it. The high cheekbones, the long-lashed eyes, moulded lips, straight nose and chiselled jawline added up to something straight out of Pel's fantasies. The body matched the face. There were no scars on the smooth skin, which was surprising. The man had no injuries anywhere other than the ones Leithia had healed. She was good at it that not a scar was visible where they had been. The man had long hair curling at the ends, framing their face in perfect waves.

*Stop drooling over him. You're supposed to be doing your chores.*

And yet, Pel found his eyes straying to the man even as he went about his household tasks.

Pel hoped that Leithia would be able to sell enough charms to buy food and medicines for the stranger as well. There were always people in need of some luck or protection, and their charms had never failed. Yet, the villagers often haggled and cursed, which was why Pel and Leithia both preferred the markets on the mainland.

Was it even safe for them to go there? Pel felt no different from before, but he remembered his skin knitting together, his magic singing in his blood, and Serityl's chorus of victory. But she had attempted her best to drown this stranger.

Pel gave the man another look. What was they doing so far out in the ocean? Where had they come from? They had been wearing some weird robe over their tunic and breeches, and all were shredded to pieces which made it even more mysterious that he didn't have more injuries on him. How had they got there? The two pieces of wood Pel had seen could hardly be sufficient for navigating the waters, but if there had been more, a ship or a boat, it had been swallowed by the ocean.

There was also the weather. The storm had started so suddenly, as soon as Leithia's vision had ended, and it had ended as soon as they were back on land, the sky a clear blue without a single cloud, and the ocean as calm as it could be. Nothing about it was natural. Pel was certain that the storm had been Serityl's doing, but why did she want to kill this man?

The man groaned, and Pel stared at them. They shouldn't have been waking up so early, but then Pel was no healer, so he couldn't really say what was normal and what was not. The man hadn't even had a fever or a cold, from what he could tell. Everything about them was unusual. Was they having magic? Did they have a spell to protect him? If so, it didn't do much. If Pel and Lithia hadn't got to them, they definitely would have drowned.

He went to the man, peering at them. The room wasn't dark, but he hadn't opened the drapes on the windows, not letting in the sunlight and it was dim.

The man opened his eyes, lids fluttering, and his gaze was

hazy and confused.

"Where... where am I?" the man asked, their voice scratchy.

"Philos," Pel replied. "Let me bring you some water."

The stranger drank the water greedily. "Thank you," they said, their voice stronger now, and eyes clear. "How am I in Philos?"

"There was a storm," Pel replied. "You nearly drowned. Do you remember?"

Their eyes focussed on Pel's face. "You saved my life."

It was a statement, and Pel nodded.

"Didn't know you were trying to kill yourself," he said, playfully, smiling at the man.

*I'm an idiot. This is why Leithia is the one to go to the market every day. I don't even know how to talk to people!*

The man smiled back. "I wasn't," they said. "Thank you for saving me, and I'm sorry I was such a bother."

"It was no problem," Pel said. "What's your name? Where are you from? And what were you doing so far out?"

The man grimaced. "I'm Belthin, male," he said. "I'm from a bit far away. An island called Behyn that's so far away it will take days to reach on a calm sea. I wasn't expecting the storm, you see. It swept me so far off my course. I was trying to go to Nagir."

"Way off course," Pel nodded. "You can go overland, if you wish to. Nagir is around four weeks' journey from here by land, though. By sea, it should take around two weeks."

"It's..." the man sighed. "I don't think it will do any good now. It was..." he sighed again, and there was so much deep sorrow in his sigh. "I had to reach there on time, you see, and I didn't, so... I don't think it will make any difference. I think I'll go home as soon as I'm able."

28

"When are you supposed to reach Nagir?" Pel asked, wanting to help despite the dangers of using his powers, especially now that he knew that the Gods themselves would want to harm him and Leithia.

"The first of Kytron," he said. "What is today?"

"The 18th of Jetron," Pel said. "The first of Kytron is ten days away."

"I don't think there's any possibility of my reaching Nagir by then, is there?"

There was an utter hopelessness in the question, coupled with desperation. Pel wished he had a better answer to give.

"I don't think so, no. Do you have magic?"

Magic was taboo in many places, but not in Philos. Nagir on the other hand... Going there by portal might be the worst idea, but Pel was feeling reckless.

Belthin shook his head. "No, no magic, I'm afraid. Why? Can magic help?"

"Magic is banned in Nagir," Pel said. "If they see you using magic, they'll probably kill you. What is the urgency, anyway? Why must you get to Nagir in time?"

"You know the festival of Utfer in Nagir?" Belthin asked.

Pel's face twisted in revulsion despite himself. Of all the Gods of Beltoros, Utfer was the worst, the most bloodthirsty, and the people of Nagir worshipped him. The festival concluded with a human sacrifice. In the olden days before the King unified Beltoros, the warriors of Nagir would go forth to capture able-bodied men from the surrounding towns and villages for the sacrifice. But the king had put a stop to such expeditions.

"I know of it," Pel said. "What of it?"

"I'm the sacrifice this year," Belthin said simply.

Pel stared at the man, aware that his mouth was hanging open. All desire that he had to help Belthin reach Nagir on time

29

was gone.

*That explains his physical perfection.*

The sacrifice had to be perfect in order to please Utfer.

"You volunteered to be sacrificed?" he asked, indignant.

The King had insisted that the sacrifices had to be volunteers, and that they had to come from Nagir.

"I had no choice," he said. "The island I come from.... we're far off, but we've always been a part of the Nagir province... no one actually asked our opinion when they made it so, and... the warriors of Nagir and the priests of Utfer threatened to kill everyone on the island if they didn't send a sacrifice. We've been sending sacrifices to Nagir every year for the last ten years. But this year... I don't know what to do." He raised pleading black eyes to Pel, a plea in them. "Can you help me?"

"Why didn't you inform the King's garrison? Surely there's one on your island?"

"You think the King would risk a rebellion in Nagir for a small island of no worth?" Belthin's voice was harsh. "There's no garrison on the island. There's only the warriors of Nagir!"

Pel digested this slowly. "Is magic banned on your island too?"

Belthin nodded. "We're all forced to eat the suppressants from early childhood. No magic manifests in our children."

"Look," Pel said. "I don't know what I can do to help, but all I know is that I can't help you to your death. Besides, you're in no condition to travel. Wait till you regain your strength. I will also consult with my sister. We will find a way by the time you get back on your feet."

"I'm fine," Belthin said as he tried to sit up, but pressed his hand on his temple, wincing. "Why does it hurt so much?"

"You need rest," Pel said. "Just trust me, all right?"

Belthin lay back down, nodding. "All right."

Pel wished he knew what to do, how to help. He wasn't opening a portal, so Belthin could get sacrificed. He had to find out why Belthin was so insistent. It didn't sound like he believed in Utfer, so it was likely that the priests or warriors were holding someone he cared for hostage.

No wonder Serityl had tried to drown him. She must hate all the Gods, and a sacrifice to one must be equally repugnant. But they had been sending sacrifices for a decade, according to Belthin, and Serityl hadn't tried to harm any of the others. It made no sense.

But one thing Pel knew was that as soon as Leithia was home, they would devise a plan to help Belthin. Not to get him to Nagir, but to get him home, and to help his people. Serityl would let them travel the ocean in peace. She might even help them get there faster than usual. Perhaps it would be best to leave Belthin behind. What if Serityl tried to drown him again?

Pel wished Serityl would tell him why she tried to drown him. Would she if he asked? Should he? What had he to lose, anyway?

"I'll be back in a bit," he told Belthin. "I won't be far. Don't try to move or stand. Do you need water or food?"

"No," he smiled at Pel. "You haven't told me your name yet."

"Pelthiel," Pel said. "Male. My sister is Leithia. We live here and she was the one who healed you."

Belthin smiled again. "Then I must thank her when I see her," he said.

# SIX

Leithia was tired by the end of the day, though she knew it was most probably because of their adventure the previous day. At least, they had saved the man. She counted out the coins she had earned that day. That should be enough to buy medicines for their guest, some meat, as well as beads, yarn and thread, and the metal pieces required to make more charms. It was fortunate that they had enough shells, thanks to Serityl's bounty.

She knew that she had risked both Pel and herself the previous day, but how could she have let someone die? What was the purpose of having magic if they couldn't even use it to save someone's life? Mostly her visions had showed her things which made no sense. There was a sacrificial altar in one, and a burning city in another. The ocean closing over her head was a frequent vision, though it was the first time she had been able to see a person as well.

She should be happy that they could save the stranger, but she didn't. Unease was all she could feel, coiled around her so tight that she thought she would suffocate from it.

Why was she feeling so uneasy?

Leithia trusted these feelings she had. That storm wasn't natural. She had felt it out there, the rage of the ocean, the fury of some power that was stronger than her magic, and all that was directed at the stranger they had saved. Who was the stranger, and why was the ocean trying to kill him?

After what happened to her father, and that last warning by her mother, the last thing she wanted was to be in the sights of the Gods. The Gods of Beltoros weren't a kindly lot. They were petty and jealous and cruel. Had she exposed herself and her brother to their wrath by saving someone they had wanted dead? If not for Pel, she wouldn't have minded; would in fact have enjoyed thumbing her nose at them, but there was Pel, and she didn't want him in any danger.

She tied up the coins in a pouch and attached it to her belt. As she walked towards the butcher's shop, her mind was still busy with speculation. There were things older than the Gods, more powerful. The power in her bloodline, the power her father had, the power they had given the world, what everyone called magic, was one such thing, which was why the Gods mistrusted it so. The Gods' power was not magic, but it was kin, and yet they mistrusted magic. Nay, hated it, and they feared anyone who was powerful in it. She could only hope that they had not noticed Pel yesterday. For there was no doubt in her mind that Pel was more powerful than her now, more powerful than even their father had been, if Serityl was to be believed. What would the Gods do to Pel if they found out?

"The usual, Leithia?" Adronis asked, as he started cutting the large slab of meat into smaller chunks, removing the fat and sinew, leaving only the choicest pieces for her.

"Yes, please." She gave him an abstracted smile.

"Something bothering you, Leit?" he asked as he weighed

33

the meat and wrapped it in a brethol leaf.

She looked at his face, at the concern reflected on it. Adronis had been their mother's friend and had been a frequent visitor to their house when she had been a child. He had often helped her out in times of scarcity, lending her money and always giving her the best pieces of meat, even when she couldn't afford them. He had also arranged for Pel and her to continue their schooling after their mother's death, brushing aside all her protestations.

She didn't know how much he knew about their father and what had led them here. But she had to tell someone.

"Something happened yesterday," she said. "Pel... his magic... I don't think anyone I've seen is so powerful, Adronis..."

There was a hard look on his face as he looked towards the horizon. "Then you hide him. Use your head, girl. There has to be a way to hide him from those bloodsuckers who call themselves Gods!"

His voice was harsh.

She drew a deep breath, glad that she had chosen to confide in Adronis. He was right. Magic was the answer. She could make a charm of concealment and have Pel wear it. Leithia might have to tell him the rest of the truth, but would that be so bad? She hadn't told him because she had deemed it best if he didn't know. What was the point, anyway? Their father was dead, and the truth would only have destroyed Pel's peace, as it did hers.

Even now, she wasn't sure telling him everything was the best option. What if he wanted revenge? But did she have a choice? His safety depended on him knowing. That way, the Gods couldn't catch him unawares as they did their father and his siblings.

"I'll do that," she said, taking the pouch of coins. "Thank

you. How much do I owe you?"

"Keep the money," he said gruffly. "You children need it more. You should do something about that beach as well."

Leithia knew from experience that arguing would do no good. She thanked him and moved away, going to the herbalist's shop. She would need to stock up on the potions for cough and cold and also to heal injuries and replenish strength. The potions purchased, she paid the herbalist and put the bottles in her basket, on top of the meat, and started the long walk home. Her mother had loved the ocean which was why her father had built their house on top of those cliffs overlooking the ocean when he felt they would need a refuge away from the mainland.

The beach was the safest place for them, for all Adronis' worry. Serityl would never let anyone come near them to harm them.

There was the stranger whom she had tried to drown, and whom they had saved. Leithia felt her breath punch out of her chest. What if the man meant to harm them? What if that was why she felt so uncomfortable? For all that, could she afford to mistrust him because of conjecture? Lithia knew well that Serityl was not fully in her right mind. She could have been getting angry for no reason. She had refused to answer Leithia's questions the previous night, singing about how powerful Pel was, and how glorious it was.

The path to their house was well worn and smooth from her almost daily trudge, and she hurried her steps as she saw that it was nearing sunset. She didn't want Pel to worry about her. He would have prepared dinner by now, and they could salt the meat and dry it tomorrow. A preservation spell would keep it good till then.

Pel was outside, watering their vegetable garden. The relief she felt at seeing him was so strong it left her giddy. She almost ran the rest of the way, but he had already seen her. He came towards her, his long strides bringing him to her side quickly, and he took the basket from her.

"We could fry some of the meat," he told her. "And salt and dry the rest. What took you so long, Leit?"

"I was..." she shook her head. "We need to talk, Pel. There's something I need to tell you."

"And there's something I need to tell you," he said. "While Belthin's still asleep. That's the name of the man we saved. He came to briefly and told me a few things."

Leithia suppressed a sigh. It was evident Pel was not going to have any peace till he had spilled out whatever was on his mind. It was better to let him. That way, she could get him to really listen when she spoke.

"Tell me," she said, taking his arm, and leading him onto the beach. She was relieved that Belthin was still asleep, though she couldn't explain even to herself why.

# SEVEN

P el couldn't blame Leithia for her caution. She had refused to let him tell her anything inside the house, taking him to the beach instead. Pel told her what Belthin had told him, and Leithia frowned.

"You believe him?"

Pel stared at her. "Why shouldn't I?"

"Because Serityl tried very hard to kill him," Leithia said. "And that should be something we needed to be careful about."

"You were the one who wanted to save him," Pel said, rather bewildered. "I know that Serityl tried to kill him, but should we judge him by that alone?"

"We know who Serityl is," Leithia said. "We know she wouldn't be trying to harm someone for no reason."

"You said it was all conjecture," he reminded her. "Maybe Serityl is indeed our aunt, and she wants to protect us, but thousands of people die in shipwrecks and storms out in the ocean, Leit. Does it mean they're all in league with the Gods? That's what you're afraid of, isn't it? That Belthin is allied with the Gods?"

Leithia pressed her lips together and stared out into the ocean. "I wish she would tell me why she tried to kill him," she said. "It's not that I don't trust him because she tried to kill him, it's just... I don't know, I just have this terrible fear whenever I'm near him."

It was Pel's turn to frown. "Why didn't you tell me that before?" he asked. There was something about how Leithia got these feelings, the same as her visions. Pel trusted them, and her, and certainly over a stranger he had met only the previous day.

"I don't know," she muttered. "I know that there has to be a reason, but Pel... you know how it is... Belthin can be completely innocent and yet cause us to be in danger... I don't want to judge someone for no reason... but... I'm so afraid."

Pel understood it. "You said you had something to tell me," he said, attempting to divert her attention. "Was it this?"

Leithia swallowed and shook her head. She looked torn. "No, it was... Pel... I didn't want to tell you, but I think you should know."

Pel felt cold somehow. "What is it, Leit?"

"When... when Mother became pregnant, Father had an augur come to tell your future. He didn't believe it, but... well, the one who came... he was different." Leithia shivered and hugged herself. "He frightened me. Mother told me to stay in my room, but I listened at the door, and... I never understood what it meant, but I remember his words, and then Father followed him outside, and asked him what he wanted..."

"Who was he?" Pel asked.

"Father called him Zeityl," she said, and Pel's breath caught.

"The God?"

She nodded. "He said... he said every word he spoke was true and that... he said he won't tell anyone about where Father is, but he should know that the other Gods will find him sooner or later, and Zeityl won't be able to protect him, even for you."

"Even for me?" Pel frowned. "What does that mean?"

"Zeityl said while he was reading your fortune that you... you were both his destiny and his end, that you would cause destruction and also bring salvation, that you would end the Gods and free the men of Beltoros, and that the Gods will always target you."

"And did Father or Mother say anything about it ever?" Pel asked.

She shook her head. "Father told Zeityl that he can't trust him to keep secrets and I think he cast a spell or something, because he told Mother later that we won't have to worry about Zeityl."

Pel digested it in silence. "What does that even mean?" he asked. "His destiny and his end? That I would—" He shook his head. "I just want to live my life, Leit. That's all. I don't want to cause destruction or bring salvation, or end the Gods."

"I know," she said. "I was hoping I would never need to tell you about it, but... I don't know, Pel... with everything happening, I thought you needed to know this as well."

He couldn't fault her for that, or for not telling him till now. "Father must have caused Zeityl to lose his memories of us if he was so certain we wouldn't need to fear him," Pel said. "But that would mean that none of the Gods likely know about the fortune that was read. So maybe they would leave us alone?"

"I want to believe that's true as well," Leithia said. "But in case... anyway, you needed to know, so you will be careful, Pel."

"I don't know just how careful we can be with the Gods after us," Pel muttered, staring out into the ocean, his ears full of Serityl singing about his power.

"We've to try," Leithia said. "But that means that if we're

to help Belthin, we can't be directly involved, Pel. Not if he's a sacrifice to Utfer. If Utfer already has his eyes on him, then our trying to help can only put us in danger."

"I understand that," Pel said. "But Leit... we can't not help."

Leithia sighed. "No," she said. "We have to. How about I go to the garrison when I go to the mainland the next and see if they can help? If Belthin wakes up, we can ask him where his island is located so we can get there."

Pel felt relief sweep through him. "You'll do that?"

"Of course," Leithia said. "I did save him, after all. It would be a shame to let him die now, for no reason."

Pel smiled at his sister, more relieved than he dared to express.

# EIGHT

Leithia left early the next morning without telling Pel or waiting for Belthin to wake. She had been restless all night, and she couldn't bear it for one more moment. Whatever was to come, they would deal with it, but for now, she had to put her mind at ease regarding Belthin. Pel had told her the name of his island home, and that would have to be enough. Surely the garrison would have heard of it.

She couldn't explain her reluctance to tell Pel where she was going. She didn't want to say anything within earshot of Belthin, even if the man was asleep or unconscious. Dragging Pel to the beach so early in the morning would have made Belthin suspicious if he woke.

Besides, she didn't want to tell her brother to keep more secrets. Pel wasn't really suited to lie or deceive, even to protect himself. It was something she both loved and despaired of. Telling him everything she had was already an enormous risk, but she knew him well enough to know that he wouldn't be blurting out anything to Belthin.

Adronis was awake and doing his morning exercises in

front of his house when she got there.

"Leithia," he said, losing the pose he was holding and wiping his chest and arms with a towel. "What brings you here so early? Is it Pel? Is he okay?"

"Everything is fine, Adronis. I want to go to the mainland for some business, and I wondered if your boat was free."

The only other boat belonged to Hadrin, the alchemist. While Leithia wasn't afraid of him, as many others were, she was not eager to go to him either.

"Oh," Adronis looked contrite. "I'm sorry, Leithia, but it was taken by Darien just last afternoon."

"It's all right," she smiled at him. The name never failed to make her wince, but she had learned to hide it. Darien was the grocer, and his trips usually lasted a couple of days. "I'll ask Hadrin."

"Do you want me to come with you?" Adronis asked.

"No, Adronis, it's okay. I know the way," she said, smiling again. "Thank you, though."

"Be careful," Adronis said.

"I will be," Leithia promised.

Hadrin was mixing some chemicals in one of the glass bottles when she got to his workshop, which was where he usually was till it was time to open his shop.

"I'll wait," Leithia said, standing judiciously away, knowing what sometimes happened with Hadrin's experiments.

Hadrin stared at her. "Don't," he said, and snapped a finger, causing the bottle itself to vanish. "Whatever you're going to do today, don't."

Leithia stared at him in bewilderment. "What?"

"There's a shadow on you," he said. "And it's not friendly. You should go back, Leithia."

Leithia stared at him. She had heard that Hadrin

sometimes saw things, and that they always came true. She felt cold, but gathered her courage and asked, "What do you see, Hadrin? What is that shadow?"

He looked away, confirming her suspicion.

"Am I going to die?" she asked, somehow calm despite everything.

"I don't know," he said, and he sounded torn. "I only see... I'm no augur... I don't know the meaning of what I see... it's... it's a warning, Leithia..."

She shook her head. "You know what you see are never simply warnings," she said. "It has never happened that what you saw didn't happen... so, whatever I do or don't doesn't really matter."

Hadrin was staring at her with something like wonder in his gaze. "Why aren't you angry?" he asked. "Or afraid? Everyone else is."

She almost laughed. "You're not responsible for what you see, Hadrin," she said. "You don't create your visions. You only see them."

She didn't tell him she had visions, too. This wasn't about her, anyway.

"Not everyone sees it that way," Hadrin said, sounding tired. "They act as if it is my fault somehow... I've tried not saying anything, but I... I can't help it..."

She understood that as well. "Well, if I'm going to die, I'm going to die," she said briskly. "We all must die someday, anyway. Can you lend me your boat? I want to go to the mainland."

"I feel like I shouldn't," he muttered. "Leithia, what I saw... it may not even happen soon."

"I know," she said. There was once an instance when what Hadrin saw happened years later. She was still a child and didn't understand most of it. Looking at Hadrin, at the lines on his face, she had a feeling that he hadn't either. He was not much older than her, after all.

Compassion stirred in her.

"Do you want a hug?" she asked.

Hadrin stared at her as if she had grown another head before stepping closer and enveloping her in a tight hug. He smelled of leather and something astringent that caused her nose to prickle and her eyes to water.

"I'm so sorry," he said.

"It's fine," she said, her voice muffled by his tunic. "It's not your fault."

"I feel like it is," he whispered.

"It's not." She stepped back, and he let her go. "So, boat?"

He nodded. "It's at the harbour. You can take it."

She gave him another smile, which he returned hesitantly.

"Thank you, Leithia," he said. "And you don't have to pay me the rent for the boat."

"But–" she began to protest, but he shook his head, a mulish look much resembling Pel's crossing his face.

"No," he said. "I cannot... Leithia, you don't know how much your kindness means... you can't understand how much it helps me every time you come to hire my boat when everyone is afraid even to look at me... and today... you should have cursed me, but instead... this is all I can do to repay you. Take the boat, and no need to pay me at all."

She wished she had more to give him, but all she had were words, and while it seemed useless to her, he didn't seem to agree.

"I meant what I said," she said. "It's not your fault, Hadrin. What you see is not on you."

She turned and walked to the harbour, not allowing Hadrin's words to haunt her. If she thought of it, she wouldn't have the strength to do anything. Besides, it was possible that it referred to something that could happen years from now. No need to worry about it yet. Right now, she had to get to the mainland and the garrison. She only hoped that they would be willing to help. After all, if Belthin was telling the truth, this was something the soldiers needed to know. Nagir shouldn't be allowed to terrorise all others, especially villages that were far-flung. Even if Belthin's island was part of Nagir, Nagir was now part of the kingdom, and the King had to ensure that they obeyed the rules and laws that he set down. The garrison had to ensure that they didn't violate any terms.

Leithia's knowledge of history was as extensive as that of any scholar, and she could quote verbatim all the terms of the surrender of Nagir. Whatever hadn't been taught at school had been supplemented by her own reading, and she was confident that she could present a good case for the garrison's intervention.

If Belthin's tale was true.

If it wasn't–

She had left Pel alone with him, and she wasn't sure she could open a portal home if Belthin happened to be lying. Portals didn't work over bodies of water. She would have to wait till they were back on their island. She most ardently hoped that Belthin was telling the truth, that she and Pel were safe, that she was not being paranoid.

The boat was where it usually was. It was well maintained, though the paint had begun to fade. It used to be a light blue, but now it was faded to almost grey. Leithia climbed on to it, untied the rope tying it to one of the poles, pulled up the ballast, and pushed off. Once away from the harbour and out in the ocean, she could use her magic and let Serityl carry her to her destination. She didn't want to let anyone see her using magic or to realise that she wasn't steering or that the boat would go against the wind.

Pel could likely do this with just a thought, but she was not Pel. But no matter how powerful he was, her brother was still naïve, and she feared for him. She didn't know what she would do if something happened to Pel.

Hadrin had seen the shadow of death on her, though. How was Pel going to feel if something happened to her? Leithia resolved to be careful and to not let anything happen to her if she could help it.

That was all she could do, anyway.

# NINE

Leithia's words were still on his mind as Pel woke up and found that his sister was gone. He looked at the sleeping form of Belthin, and wondered if the man was truly an enemy. He hoped not, but anyway, they would know when Leithia went to the garrison next week. She must have gone early to the village market today. Pel wished he could help more, but he was never comfortable around people, and Leithia knew it.

Hadrin had once told Pel that he saw something, but he wasn't sure what. It looked like a shadow and a halo all at once. Pel knew that Hadrin had something similar to a prophetic sight, but sometimes what he saw was really cryptic. When their meaning was clear, people feared him. When their meaning wasn't clear, they were angry with him.

Hadrin was no augur. He could only see; he had no idea what it meant, very like Leithia with her visions. Sometimes he knew what the things he saw meant, like death or fire or gold. Sometimes, like what he saw on Pel, it made no sense. And yet, people weren't ready to accept it. They wanted to know, and when they knew, they blamed him, as if he had caused what he

47

saw. It made no sense to Pel. Hadrin wasn't responsible for what he saw any more than Leithia was for her visions. It was pointless to blame either of them.

Pel went outside to weed and water their gardens. It was frustrating to have so much magic and yet not be able to help his sister earn them a living. He could do repairs and gardening and fishing, but that was all. Serityl was abundant with her bounty to their nets, but it had never occurred to Pel or Leithia to sell any extra they had. They would give it away to those who needed it, or trade it for something they needed. Sometimes they salted and stored the extra fish.

Could he perhaps come up with a preservation spell that would keep the fish and meat fresh? That would have been useful. Pel had never heard of a spell like that, and had no idea how to make one, but he wanted to try all the same.

A whimper from inside the house made him look up from the patch of earth he was fertilising. Was Belthin awake? He put aside the basket of manure and got up, stretching to ease his cramped muscles from crouching so long. He hadn't even had breakfast, and it was already midday.

Again, a sound from inside the house. Pel went to the bucket of water by the door to wash up before entering the house. Belthin was asleep, but was moving around in his sleep, words in some unfamiliar language spilling from his lips, and occasional whimpers as well.

"Belthin," Pel said, kneeling next to him. He touched his shoulder gently. "Belthin, wake up."

Belthin's eyes opened suddenly, and he looked at Pel with a fear that was almost animalistic. Pel flinched back, and Belthin blinked, the fear replaced by confusion.

"Pelthiel?"

Pel removed his hand. "You looked like you were having a

nightmare," he said. "Are you okay? Do you need anything?"

Belthin looked at him, something strange in his expression. "No, I'm fine... I... did I say anything?"

"Nothing I can understand," Pel said. "You seemed to be muttering in some language I don't know."

Belthin sat up and brushed a hand across his wet eyes. "I'm fine," he said. "It was just a bad dream."

"I'm sorry," Pel said. "Do you need a hug?"

"What?" Belthin stared at him, confusion on his face.

"My sister hugs me whenever I have nightmares," Pel explained. "I do the same for her. It makes us feel better. Has no one hugged you? You seem so confused."

Belthin looked away, cheeks staining crimson. "We're not too great on physical affection back home," he said.

"It's all right," Pel said gently. "It's not for everyone."

Belthin turned to him. "Will you hug me?" he asked. "I want to know what it's like."

"Sure," Pel said, leaning over to hug him, but Belthin overbalanced and they both fell on to the mattress, Pel on top, their faces close, so close that Pel could see the faint smattering of freckles on Belthin's face, and smell him. He should have smelled of sweat, but instead, there was the fragrance of something sharp, something that reminded Pel of the storm they had rescued him from.

"You have freckles," he said, chuckling.

"You're beautiful," Belthin said at the same time.

Pel felt his cheeks burn. "So are you," he said. He had thought that from the first moment he had seen him.

"Pelthiel," Belthin said. "I... may I kiss you?"

Pel swallowed, but for some reason, he couldn't look away. He was attracted to Belthin, but the man was still not well, and Pel–

49

"I think maybe we shouldn't just yet," he said, rising, and getting off the bed. "Wait till you're strong enough to not fall down from a hug. After all, with you this weak, a kiss may cause something worse."

Belthin laughed, his cheeks red, making the freckles stand out more. "Pelthiel," he said. "I like you."

Pel smiled at him. "I like you too. My sister and I will help you. Don't worry, all right?"

"Where is she?" Belthin asked, sitting up again, this time leaning against the wall.

"Gone to the market to see the stuff she makes," Pel said, moving to the kitchen. "I'll make you some soup, and afterwards, you should rest."

Belthin said nothing, and Pel busied himself in chopping the vegetables and cutting the meat. He couldn't help imagining what it would be like to kiss Belthin. Pel had never kissed anyone. Had Belthin? He didn't sound like he had, but what did Pel know, anyway?

His thoughts moved to the Gods again. Did they know of him? Were they planning to attack him and Leithia? Pel wondered if Serityl would tell him anything if he asked. She talked to Leithia, but not that much to Pel. She had told him her name, and had sung to him, but she had never answered any of his questions.

He tried not to imagine the state she was in, constantly chained to the waters. Pel might choose to stay here for eternity if it meant he could be safe from the Gods, but could he ask that of Leithia? She wanted to travel, and Pel had been saving up for that.

He added the stock and stirred mechanically. Would Leithia be safer without him? Would the Gods leave her alone or did they want to exterminate everyone in their bloodline? The latter seemed more likely.

A sound made him turn his head, and he saw Belthin at the door to the kitchen.

"I feel better," Belthin said. "And that smell was too good, so I thought I'll come have a look."

"It'll be ready soon," Pel said, turning back to add herbs and spices and salt, and stirred again. "You can sit down."

He felt Belthin at his back. "It was nice," he said. "The hug. May I hug you, Pelthiel?"

"As long as you don't jolt me too much," Pel said lightly, though his heart was hammering.

Belthin hugged him from behind, his breath tickling Pel's ear. "The soup looks and smells good," he said. "Is there anything you're not good at, Pelthiel?"

Pel laughed. "Lots of things," he said, as he held out the spoon to Belthin for a taste. "You have to let go now. I need to remove it from the stove."

Belthin released him, and Pel missed his warmth, but he had work to do.

"You look troubled," Belthin said, sitting down at the kitchen table.

"Just thinking," Pel said as he carried the soup to the table. He returned to douse the flames of the stove and carried bowls, ladles, and spoons to the table. He served soup for Belthin first before taking some for himself. "About the Gods. Do they even care about us?"

Belthin blew on his soup before eating. "This is delicious," he said. "And as for the Gods, I don't know... from everything I've seen, though, I doubt they care. Why should they?"

"You mean all the tales about them deriving power from our prayers are just nonsense?" Pel asked. "Because otherwise, I should think they ought to care, at least so they would have power."

"I don't know," Belthin said. "But even if they don't care, people care for them, and they believe in them, and worship them, so again, why should the Gods care?"

"People are afraid of them," Pel muttered. "Isn't that wrong? People shouldn't be afraid of Gods... they should be able to care or not... I don't know... I don't like the Gods very much, I'm afraid."

Belthin chuckled. "You don't know them either," he said. "And yet you've already got so many opinions on them, and none of them favourable."

Pel frowned. "Do you like them? After how you've been treated because of them?"

"It's not Utfer's fault that the priests and the people of Nagir are so nasty," Belthin said.

"Isn't it?" Pel asked. "He can just say he doesn't want human sacrifices. Looks to me that you've some prejudices yourself."

Belthin looked startled. He chuckled. "Maybe I do, but... you know, we've spent our whole lives worshipping them... it's difficult to get rid of those habits."

"Not good habits," Pel said, shaking his head. "But I get it. I mean... probably my prejudices come from old habits too. Have you heard of a God called Zeityl?"

Belthin's face went pale. "It's not allowed to speak his name," he said, voice hushed. "No one but the priests are aware of it even... where did you hear it, Pelthiel?"

Pel frowned. "Some book," he said, which was true anyway. "Why? What is so special about him?"

Belthin shook his head. "I don't know... the priests... they don't allow questions... They just... all I know is that he's the most powerful God there is, and that even the other Gods listen to him... he...he... he's like their leader, though he doesn't care for it."

"Looks like you know a lot," Pel said quietly, but he was troubled as well. If what Belthin said was true, Pel's father had managed to spell the most powerful of Gods to forget about him.

"Why do you ask?" Belthin asked.

"Because I saw the name, and there wasn't any information," Pel said, almost absently, though his heart was hammering. Zeityl had said Pel was his destiny and his destruction. What did that mean? Pel was tired of all the cryptic things that seemed to revolve around him.

"Pelthiel?" Belthin asked. "Are you all right?"

Pel nodded. "I am." He smiled at the other man. "I'll wash up. You should rest."

"I don't want to," Belthin said. "I want to help, please."

Pel nodded. "I'll wash and you can dry," he said, collecting the bowls and spoons. He would leave the rest of the soup for Leithia when she came home.

Belthin stood too close to him, and the glances he gave from time to time were very distracting. As soon as they were finished Pel turned to the other man, boldly stepping into his space, and cupping his face.

"Going to kiss you now," he said, his heart pounding madly against his ribcage.

Belthin's lips crashed on his, and Pel was pulled closer to the hard body, and it felt amazing. Pel wasn't sure if he was doing it right, but from the reaction he could feel against his thigh, he probably was.

"Pel," Belthin sounded wrecked. "What... I..."

Pel leaned his forehead against the other man's. "More?" he asked.

"If I do, I may want more," Belthin whispered.

"So do I," Pel said, thrusting against Belthin to prove his

53

point.

"I've not done this before," Belthin said. "What if I hurt you?"

"That makes two of us," Pel said. "We'll figure it out together, okay? You won't hurt me."

"Pel," Belthin said before kissing him again, and this time Pel didn't have time to think as he got lost in the kiss.

# TEN

The captain of the guards looked at Leithia as if she was mad. "What are you talking about?" he demanded. "There's no such place. When the King conquered Nagir, he brought all its provinces, island ones included, under his rule. There's no island without a garrison, and the one you speak of... as far as I know, that's uninhabited."

Leithia felt her heart sink. "Are you certain?" she asked. "I don't want to accuse someone without any proof."

"Of course I'm certain," the captain sounded offended. "But if you want to have proof, I can send someone there, and you can go with them. You'll have to take a couple of our mages along, to make certain that both of you get there safely and back."

"How long would it take?" Leithia asked.

"A week usually," the captain said. "To get there. Another week to return. If the weather holds fair. Our weather mage can maybe save you a few days, but don't expect to be back before ten days at least."

Ten days to two weeks. She would have to leave Pel alone

55

for that time, leave him with Belthin, no less. Leithia felt trapped. She should go home, tell Pel what she learned, but there was still the niggling doubt in her mind.

What if Belthin was telling the truth? What if the captain didn't know about the island and Belthin's people there? Would Leithia condemn an innocent man and his villagers out of hearsay?

"All right," she said, resolved. "But I would need to send a message to my brother."

"One of my messengers can take it," the captain said. "Just give it to them."

Leithia nodded. She wouldn't tell Pel where she was, but she would tell him that she would be away for a few days. The messengers employed by the garrison were civilians, and had no uniform, so neither Pel nor Belthin would realise she had gone to the garrison just yet. If Belthin was lying, it would be better for him to not know, and if he wasn't, there was no harm done, anyway.

The message written and sealed, she waited for the captain to arrange a boat, and the weather mage and a warrior mage. There was no need for a weather mage since Serityl would never harm her, but she couldn't tell anyone that. She hoped that nothing would happen that would bring their secret out in the open.

Everyone worshipped the Gods, and the Gods could use anyone to harm them. There were a few rare people who would defy the Gods for them, but for the majority who didn't know them, whatever the Gods commanded would be their decree. Even if they knew them and believed they were evil, most people were so afraid of the Gods that they would obey them without thought.

Leithia had very little hopes that Pel's little display would have gone unnoticed, but she could always hope. But if the Gods' attention was going to fall on them because of that, Belthin had to be telling the truth and couldn't be an agent of the Gods. Something within her relaxed, but she still couldn't forget her mistrust and fear.

As their boat finally left the docks, Leithia felt her heart ease somewhat. For better or for worse, she would know the truth soon. Besides which was the swooping feeling she had every time she was in the ocean. She could imagine that she was travelling to some far-off land, and going to have very many adventures.

The boat was fast and well equipped. It was more like a small ship with a small cabin where they all rested and had food. Leithia took her turn pumping the bilge because it seemed unfair to let the soldiers and mages do all the work. She apologised to Serityl in her mind for soiling the waters, but Serityl didn't seem to hear or care.

The weather remained fair, and the wind favoured them. The weather mage got all the credit, but Leithia caught the puzzled look on his face as the wind continued to be fair. He knew he wasn't doing anything, and he had no idea why this was happening.

"The weather seems good," she said. "Very pleasant here. Is it usually like this? Have you all come this way before?"

"I've been sailing these seas for a long time," the mage said. "I've never seen the sea as calm, or the wind as favourable. It is really strange. You must be bringing us good luck, lady."

Leithia remembered Hadrin's vision, and couldn't help but smile, hoping it didn't come across as too bitter. Lucky? If she was lucky, her parents would still be with her. Her brother wouldn't be in danger because she just had to save that man. She wouldn't be on this boat, looking for answers.

"I hope so," was all she answered, however. What else was there to say, anyway?

"Something strange at work here," one of the soldiers muttered. "Is this some enchantment?"

The weather mage shook his head. "The sea isn't something any mage can control. For some reason, she wants us safe today, and let's take full advantage."

Leithia couldn't have agreed more, though her thoughts kept turning to her brother. Was Pel okay? Had Belthin tried to harm him in any way? She hoped not. Even if the man was an agent of the Gods, he must have some purpose other than killing them.

If he was even capable of that. Killing humans was not easy, Leithia had heard. She hoped it was true. Not that she thought Belthin could harm Pel, who was perhaps the most powerful magic user in all Beltoros. No one but a God could take him on, but that didn't mean they had to be careless or boastful.

She dozed off and when she woke up, it was dark. The boat was still in the water, and making steady progress. She remembered what they said about it taking time. She hoped that Pel would have got her message and wouldn't be worried.

Food and water were not scarce, but everything tasted of salt and fish. Leithia had no idea why that was, but the others seemed okay with it, so she had to assume it was normal. She gathered they were making good progress and that they would be there at least a couple of days before they had expected to. Leithia whispered her thanks to Serityl before going to sleep each day and waited for the journey to end.

# ELEVEN

Pelthiel frowned as he read Leithia's message. A man had brought it to their house around midday and had left soon after. Leithia had written that she was going on a boat for a couple of weeks, an adventure. She had apologised for going off just like that, but that she felt she would never again get a chance to travel.

Pel didn't mind her going, or even how short the letter was, but he wished she had chosen another time. True, they had thought to wait a few more days and get more details from Belthin before going to the garrison, but it still seemed like a betrayal.

Except—

The festival of Utfer would be over by the time Leithia returned, and that was good, wasn't it? Because Belthin would still be here, and safe, and Pel didn't need to make any other decisions.

A small smile formed on his lips as he thought of Belthin and the night they had spent. There was still a burn to his back, but he didn't mind it. It had been new and felt so, so good. It was evident that Belthin was as much an innocent as Pel himself had been, and somehow that made it all the more special.

"Pelthiel?" Belthin asked from the door. He looked troubled. "Are you okay?"

"Yeah, just, Leithia has gone on a short trip, she says," Pel put the letter inside his tunic pocket, and picked up the trowel again. "I hope she's okay."

"What are you doing?" Belthin asked.

"Replanting some of our vegetables," Pel said. "I need to weed a bit after this."

"Can't you use magic for that?" Belthin asked.

"Yeah," Pel said. "But I like working with my hands. It doesn't feel the same to use magic. More trouble than it's worth, really. I mean, magic needs some fine control to do certain tasks, and mine aren't suited to things like gardening." He grinned at Belthin. "I can split some rocks or chop the firewood, though, or uproot a tree. But things like replanting, weeding? Nah."

Belthin's eyes held something strange, something like awe and wonder. Something that made Pel's heart race.

"Why are you looking at me like that?" he asked.

"Like what?" Belthin asked, his voice soft and quiet.

"Like you're doing now," Pel said. "Like you... I don't know... what are you thinking, anyway?"

"How amazing you are," Belthin said. "And how fortunate I am to have met you."

Pel's face burned. "I'm just another person," he said, and hated that he couldn't reveal his truth to Belthin. "Meeting me is no great fortune."

"I would disagree," Belthin said, looking away, something clouding his glance. "I thought... I hadn't known that I could be happy, that I could have someone who cared for me like you do, with no expectations... that you would fight for my life when it gains you nothing."

60

"I'm sure you have others who care for you that way, too," Pel said. "Your family? Your parents? Any siblings that you have?"

"I never knew my parents," Belthin said quietly, heavily. "My siblings... yes, they care, but they also have expectations, Pelthiel. I'm not saying they care because of that or that they would stop if I failed, but... they're my family... my blood... they have to care, I think, but you... you and your sister... you didn't have to save me, but you did... you don't have to be kind, but you are... and now the way you look at me... Pelthiel, tell me that I'm not imagining things."

"I don't know what you're seeing, so I can't tell you that," Pel said evenly, even as his heart was hammering. "But you're wrong about your family. They don't have to care for you. Families may share blood, but that doesn't mean they owe love. That's something entirely different. If they care for you, they do that on their own."

Belthin's breath shuddered. "Oh, Pelthiel," he spoke quietly. "You've no idea what you're doing to me."

Pel couldn't explain why that pleased him. "Something good, I hope," he said, smiling.

"More than," Belthin said. "I never..." He shook his head. "Never mind. I'm just being silly. You carry on, and I'll just be inside."

"All right," Pel said, though he was feeling a bit disappointed. "You should rest."

"I'm fine," Belthin said, and he looked it, with colour back on his face and no sign of tiredness. "I thought I'll help you clean today. Just show me what to do. I want to make myself useful."

"Have you never cleaned?" Pel asked.

"Never had to," Belthin sighed. "But I can learn."

"All right then, I'll show you when I'm done with this,"

Pel said. "You can rest till then."

He was both amused at Belthin's obvious ineptitude with household tasks and charmed by his desire to help.

"I don't want to rest," Belthin said, sitting down on the top step. "Is it all right if I wait here?"

"Of course," Pel said. "You know, I've been reading up on Nagir and their sacrificial practises."

Belthin tensed. "And?"

"While they do have human sacrifices every year, that's just random people, mostly criminals from their own city. But every decade or so, they hand pick someone to be their biggest offering. Somehow, that is the one that most people know about. A sacrifice who's chosen at birth and raised to be nothing else." Pel didn't look at Belthin now, focussing on uprooting the small weeds that had started to poke their way through the soil. "You are that sacrifice, aren't you?"

Belthin's breath came out in a loud exhale. "Yes."

"You do know that the sacrifice to Utfer, the big sacrifice that you're supposed to be, has to be a virgin."

"I know." This time Belthin's voice was small, a thin thread of sound.

"Is that why you slept with me?" Pel didn't look at Belthin as he asked that. Not that he would blame the other man if that had been his reason.

"Pelthiel, I..."

"It's a simple question," Pel said, sighing, and turning his face to look at Belthin. "You just need to say yes or no. It doesn't get any simpler than that."

Belthin dropped his eyes. "In part, yes. But also because I wanted to. It's not so simple for me, Pelthiel."

Pel wanted to get up and hug the other man, but refrained. "I understand you wanting to save your life," he said. "I don't blame you for it. I'm glad I could help."

Belthin rose and stalked closer to him, pulling Pel up by his arm. "Are you even listening to me?" he demanded, eyes blazing. "It wasn't just to save my life! I wanted it, Pelthiel, wanted *you!*" His voice turned husky, gaze darkening. "Still do."

Pel shrugged off the grip, and cupped Belthin's face, leaning till they were sharing air. "I'm glad," he said, and kissed him.

Belthin kissed him back, gripping Pel's shoulder with one hand, and the other holding him against his body. Not that Pel wanted to break loose. He was growing hard, and he felt Belthin's interest as well.

"We should go inside," he murmured, breaking the kiss, but not moving away. "I need to wash my hands as well. They're filthy."

"Use magic," Belthin said. "Or is that too difficult for you as well?"

Pel chuckled. "Maybe. Don't want to risk taking off my skin as well."

Belthin laughed softly, a puff of air against Pel's lips. "Is it too early to tell you that I love you?"

Pel stilled. He wasn't sure what to say. He liked Belthin, desired him, but love?

"Maybe," he said. "Belthin, this isn't me saying no, but we haven't known each other long."

"I know," Belthin said softly. "I also know that you'll say that this is because I haven't been with anyone else, that I... I haven't had any opportunity to be myself yet."

"Wouldn't that be true?" Pel asked.

"I'm not saying it isn't," Belthin said. "But from the moment I saw you, I've had this feeling that I know you... It's strange... it's... it's like I've been waiting for you and I realised it

63

only when I saw you."

Pel's breath caught. He had thought he was the only one who felt the familiarity, but apparently not.

"You felt familiar to me as well," he whispered.

Belthin leaned in till their foreheads were touching. "I'm ready to wait, Pelthiel," he murmured. "After all, I've waited all my life for you without even knowing it."

Pel kissed him.

# TWELVE

The island came into view on the fifth day, and the soldiers and mages seemed surprised. Leithia was not. She had more or less expected it. After all, Serityl had been singing in her ears for the entire journey. A crescendo of love and victory that drowned out everything else, including her fears.

Still, as they approached the deserted beach, Leithia's heart was pounding hard enough to break her ribs. As she accepted the soldier's hand to help her on to shore, her skirts held up with the other to avoid it getting wet, she felt the spike of apprehension in her gut twist and dig deeper.

The beach was entirely devoid of anything but sand, the lapping waves, and the trees swaying in the breeze beyond the shoreline. There was nothing to indicate that the island was inhabited. There were cliffs she could see at a distance, but no plumes of smoke rose from them from any fires.

They should have seen the smoke.

If there were people on this island, they would have seen smoke from chimneys, because it was the time when people would be engaged in preparing food. They would have seen boats, or children, or at least a pet animal.

Limbs shaking, she trailed after the soldier and the mages, knowing already that her fears hadn't led her astray. Pel might have felt Belthin harmless, and even familiar, but Leithia had felt only foreboding from the start. She wished she hadn't thought of saving him. It was the helplessness that had prompted her. The way her visions took her, rendering her powerless to do anything since most were never specific.

She had seen her mother's death and had been unable to do anything. The sickness that took her could not be cured, not with magic, nor with medicine. Perhaps she was trying to make up for her inability to help her mother. Perhaps she wanted some power back, some choice in her life.

Because despite her desire to see the world, to sail in the unknown seas, Leithia knew that she couldn't. Not when the Gods sought them, hunted them. Maybe not as obviously as they had done her father and his siblings, but Leithia knew that meant nothing. The Gods never forgot and they would never stop looking.

Perhaps that was why she had been so adamant about saving Belthin, because it made her feel good to make a choice, to feel in control. But it seemed that she had only invited danger into their lives and their homes. Pel had to use his powers; more, he had to reveal the full extent of it. There was no doubt in her mind that the Gods would have noticed already.

And Belthin was the catalyst, even if not the cause. But the lies he told meant that there was something more at work here. Leithia didn't yet know what, but she had to be suspicious that it was nothing good. The fear she had felt when she first saw Belthin was the right reaction. For whatever reasons, that man was dangerous, and a liar.

And she had left Pel alone with him.

Leithia knew her brother, and while she trusted his ability
to protect himself, she also knew how soft-hearted he was. He
would never bring himself to mistrust Belthin, not without any
reason or proof. He also got attached easily. If he became friends
with Belthin within this time, he would be heartbroken when he
learned her news.

But Pel had to know. It was better to know the truth and
be hurt than to live in a false paradise. Besides, Pel was smart, and
sooner or later, he would figure it out even if she kept it from
him. She could confront Belthin on her own, but Pel wasn't a
child. She didn't want to protect him from this, not if Belthin
had been sent by the Gods.

Was that why Serityl had tried to drown him?

"There's no one here," the soldier said, sounding
disgusted. "We told you. This is an uninhabited island."

"I know," she said, looking around.

"I can cast a spell," one of the mages said. He was a young
man. Darin. "It will tell us if there are any humans here, or any
magic that's keeping us from seeing them."

"Do that," the soldier said. "I don't want to spend days
looking for people who aren't here."

It was a spell Leithia knew, and it needed a lot of power. If
she wasn't hiding from people and if she wasn't determined to
keep anyone from suspecting the extent of her powers, she would
have cast it herself.

Darin took a few moments more than Leithia would have,
but he was sagging by the end of it, and shaking his head. "No
people," he said, panting. "Animals, yes, but no people, and no
magic."

"Guess we should turn back," the soldier said, rather
sourly.

"I'm sorry," Leithia felt compelled to say. "It seems I've led you on a fool's errand and wasted everyone's time."

Perversely, the soldier didn't seem to like her apologising. "It's all right, miss," he said gruffly. "We had to check it out. It's not like we have much else to do, anyway. When you go home, tell that friend of yours not to spread unnecessary tales around. Could get them into lots of trouble with Nagir if they catch wind of it."

"I'll tell them," Leithia said. She would ask Belthin why he lied, but first she would tell Pel. Letting Pel know was more important than anything else. She wished there was a way to send a message to Pel immediately.

They were all silent as they trekked back to the boat, and Leithia briefly considered asking Serityl, but discarded the notion almost immediately. As messengers went, Serityl was quite unreliable.

# THIRTEEN

Days turned into a week and two, and there was no word from Leithia. Pel was tempted to go to town and then onto the mainland to get news of her. He was more worried than he showed, but Belthin seemed to pick up on it, anyway.

"She'll be fine," he said softly. "She's powerful in magic, right?"

"In some forms of magic, yes," Pel said. "She is like... I don't know, creative? Her magic is more attuned to making things, and defensive spells. It's subtle and small, despite its power. I am more destructive, offensive, battering things down kind of magic."

Belthin looked wistful. "I don't know much about magic," he said. "Like I said, they didn't want us using it back home, and never taught us about it, either."

Anger was something Pel didn't feel often, but every time Belthin talked of his home, and his life before, that was all he felt. It was like Belthin lived in a prison where even his thoughts were regulated. He supposed it was the same for everyone on his island.

"How can you think the Gods are good after how they treated you?" he demanded.

Belthin looked uncomfortable and shrugged. "Who else do we have?" he asked in a small voice. "They kept storms away and gave us plentiful harvests. So what if they demanded some small things in return?"

"Small things?" Pel asked, furious. "They took your freedoms, your choices away! They wanted your life, Belthin! How is that a small thing?"

"What is a human life to a God?" Belthin asked, and he didn't sound bitter, not even resigned, but earnest. "They're immortals, and we will all die one day anyway, so why can't they ask us to give that short life for their powers so they can help more people?"

"Help?" Pel nearly yelled. "What they are doing is the opposite of help!"

It was no use. No matter how much they argued, Belthin would not budge. It was like he couldn't understand that the Gods were in the wrong.

For all that, Pel still liked spending time with Belthin, enjoyed their arguments, the hours they spent working together side by side in the garden, and the kitchen, and the house. He taught Belthin to cook, to clean, to make his bed, to weed, and to plant.

They went to market together, and Pel introduced Belthin to Adronis who didn't ask too many questions fortunately. Pel didn't volunteer too much information either, just that Belthin was someone they rescued and they were planning to send him back home when Leithia was back.

"You didn't tell him everything," Belthin remarked as they walked home.

"No," Pel agreed. "Not going to frighten away people by telling them you're a sacrifice to Utfer." Pel scowled. "I'm glad that you're still here. The festival should be over by now."

"Does it matter?" Belthin asked. "As the chosen, I can be sacrificed any day. The festival is just an event."

Pel knew it, but he didn't want to think of it now. "You're not a virgin anymore," he said. "Doesn't that make you ineligible or something?"

Belthin nodded. "It should," he said. "I hope it does, because I like being here, with you, Pelthiel. I wish I could live here with you for the rest of my life."

"So do I," Pel said, and was surprised at how much he meant it. Gone was his earlier uncertainty. Gone was the confusion about his feelings, and about Belthin's. Right now, all Pel wanted was Belthin, and to be able to live with him for the rest of his life. "I love you, Belthin."

Belthin stared at him, and his face paled. "You love me?"

Pel took a step towards him and cupped his face. "I do. But why does that make you look scared?"

Belthin's breath shuddered, and he closed his eyes, his forehead touching Pel's. "I'm scared," he said. "Scared of losing this, you... Pelthiel... I... there are a lot about me that you don't know... that I..."

"It's okay," Pel said softly. "There are things about me that you don't know, either. But we have time to get to know those things. Time to tell each other everything. You don't need to force yourself to say anything right now."

"Yeah, we have time," Belthin said softly, and kissed Pel, sweet and soft and chaste. "I love you more than I've ever loved anyone or anything, Pelthiel. I have never known it was possible to feel this way."

"Me neither," Pel said quietly. "Stay here, Belthin. Stay

with me. If Leithia isn't back by the end of the week, I'll go to the garrison myself. We'll save your people. I promise you that."

Belthin looked away, a flush on his face. "Is it bad that I don't really care?" he asked, his voice quiet. "My siblings would be fine, and I really don't care for anyone else."

Pel wasn't sure he understood it. "I am not going to tell you who you should care for or not," he said. "But I would rather they don't get hurt for no fault of theirs. The garrison can keep them safe, Belthin. Even if you don't care, it won't be right to let them be killed."

"You're too good," Belthin said quietly. "Pelthiel, you care for people you haven't even met, or seen... You rescued me when you didn't have to... you and your sister... you are good people."

Pel chuckled. "You sound like you haven't met any decent people before."

Belthin shook his head. "Perhaps I haven't. No one who is selfless, anyway. People always want something, but you and your sister... you just want to help..."

"There are a lot of people like that," Pel said softly, his heart aching. "You remember Adronis? He's also like that. There are lots more. It's not as rare a thing as you think, Belthin. Most people are good, and they want to help." He took Belthin's hand in his. "You'll see, Belthin. This world is a beautiful place, and people are good."

There was a strange look on Belthin's face as he looked at Pel, and then he pulled him closer and kissed him hard. Pel responded and was surprised that Belthin was trembling in his arms.

"I love you," Belthin said, his voice shaking. "I never want to lose you, Pelthiel."

"Why would you?" Pel asked, amused, and Belthin said nothing but hugged him, still quivering.

# FOURTEEN

Leithia saw that Pel was working in the garden as she approached the house. Her heart slowed down, and she heaved a sigh of relief. He was safe. She had worried for nothing.

Pel looked up and his eyes met hers, his face breaking into the biggest smile she had ever seen on his face.

"Leit!" he said as he hurried to her side. He caught her in a hug, holding her tight enough to bruise, tight enough to make her breathless.

"I can't breathe, Pel."

He laughed, but relaxed his grip. "I missed you," he said. "I was so worried, Leit. Where were you? How could you just go like that?"

She smiled at him. "I'm back now, aren't I? But Pel, there's something I need to tell you."

She transported them both to the beach, where Serityl's music kept prying ears out, and she hoped prying eyes as well.

"I lied," she said. "I didn't go to sail all around. I went to the garrison and to the island Belthin said he came from."

"And?" Pel looked eager, and Leithia hated that she would

73

have to burst his bubble. But she couldn't lie to Pel about this. It was too important. So, she told him everything, from what she learned at the garrison to what they found on the island.

Pel staggered back a step. "What do you mean it was uninhabited?"

"There was no one there, and I don't think it ever was inhabited. They took me to a couple of inhabited islands in that area as well, and the garrison has their soldiers there, and none of them have ever sent anyone to Nagir."

"So he lied," Pel said, his voice sounding strange and devastation writ large upon his face. "Why did he lie?"

"Pel." Leithia took a step closer to her brother. "What happened when I was gone?"

"We... we got close," Pel said, his eyes full of a grief so intense Leithia felt breathless just from looking. "I fell in love."

"Oh, Pel," Leithia's heart ached. "Let's go talk to him. Maybe there is a reasonable explanation for this. Maybe I mistook the island. Maybe there is some other reason."

Pel shook his head. "I wish it were that simple, Leit. But we both know that you're just saying this to make me feel better."

She couldn't deny that. "Pel," she said, placing a hand on his shoulder. "I'm so sorry. If I'd known... I'm sorry."

"I am too," Pel said. "But, Leit, don't be sorry that you learned the truth, and that you told me... I am glad I know."

Leithia said nothing, but pulled her brother into a hug, holding him tight, and wishing she could take away his heartache as well.

She could hope, but in the end, it was futile, and she knew it. They held each other for a while more, and the song of Serityl had taken on a soothing quality as well. Once again, Leithia had to wonder if Serityl knew what was going on. Was she truly insane or pretended to be? She chided herself for the thought.

What did she know of Serityl's pain, the pain of losing all her siblings, and then having to be bound to be part of the elements she was once mistress of? The oceans were her domain now, but she had no control over any other body of water.

Pel was the one to let go first, stepping back and scrubbing away his tears. "Let's go talk to him," he said.

Leithia nodded, and for her brother's sake, she hoped that Belthin would have an explanation. Something that would make sense, would be reasonable, something they could both accept. Leithia had never been in love, had never found anyone with whom she had wanted to spend the rest of her life, and she had never thought of what it would be like when Pel did. Now that he did, all she wanted was for him to have it, have that life, that love, that happiness.

She remembered enough of her parents' life to know that it was possible to be happy even if you were hiding from the Gods. She wanted that for her brother, who had never wanted anything for himself. Pel deserved to have it.

Their house was empty, and so were the gardens. Food was cooked and dishes done, and stacked neatly, but there was no sign of Belthin.

"Where is he?" Pel asked. "Where could he have gone? He was here when I went outside to weed the garden."

Leithia was as confused as Pel was. Had Belthin left? But why? It was then she saw the parchment, a corner sticking out from under Pel's pillow. She took it, saw that it was a folded piece bearing Pel's name, and she held it out to him.

Pel's hands were trembling as he took it and unfolded it. Leithia saw his eyes move, and his face grow pale.

"He's gone to Nagir," Pel whispered. "He said he doesn't want to bring any trouble to us, and so he has gone to Nagir."

"But the festival is over," Leithia said.

"He's The Sacrifice, Leit. Not just any sacrifice... they don't need a festival, and he's a man, so there's no way of confirming his virginity or otherwise..."

Leithia closed her eyes for just a moment, getting her breathing and heart rate under control. That explained the physical perfection of the man, but nothing else.

She opened them again, and looked at Pel. "There may be no way for people to determine, but can he fool Utfer? The God will know."

"I'm going after him," Pel said. "We don't even know that the people from Nagir are looking for him. I can't let him sacrifice himself like this, not before... I am going after him."

"We don't even know if that's where he's gone," Leithia said. "Pel, he has already lied to us. Why should this be true? If he lied about the village, what all might he have lied about? We don't know anything about him. What if the Gods sent him? What if that's why Serityl tried to drown him? What if that's why I felt afraid?"

Pel's breath shuddered, and he sank to the floor. "I love him," he whispered. "I trusted him... Why didn't he stay and explain, Leit? He said he loved me... that he wanted to spend his life with me... I believed him..."

She knelt at his side and hugged him, her chin on top of his head as she rubbed soothing circles on his back with one hand, the other stroking his head. "I'm sorry," she whispered. "I'm so sorry, Pel."

The earth shook, and the sky darkened, lighting shooting down into their garden with a deafening crash. Leithia trembled, for she remembered this from her childhood.

"The Gods are here," she whispered.

Pel freed himself from her grasp and wiped his tears. "Then let us go and face them," he said. "Let us end this, one way or another."

Leithia nodded, her face hard. "Let's," she said, rising, and Pel got up as well.

Hand in hand, they walked out of their house. Every instinct in Leithia wanted to run, but their parents had run too, and it had done no good. Sometimes, you just had to stand your ground and face your enemy.

# FIFTEEN

Pel felt strangely calm as he faced the group of people who were outside, Leithia's hand still inside his own. The Gods looked so ordinary, except for the palpable fury that radiated from them. Behind them, however...

A horde of people, and Pel recognised the crest on their armour and the flag they carried. The Warriors of Nagir. There had to be thousands, which made him wonder how their tiny island fit them all. They were in columns that stretched as far as his eyes could see.

"What do you want?" Leithia asked.

One of the Gods stepped forward. Pel didn't know who it was. "I'm Utfer," they said. "Where's Zeityl?"

Pel exchanged a confused glance with Leithia. "Are we supposed to know?"

"Stop playing games with us!" Another God shouted as they stepped forth as well. "He was here! He came, he braved that ocean, and now we can't sense him, we can't find him... What did you do to him?"

Shock kept Pel immobile, and Leithia stiffened as well. Belthin was Zeityl? The leader of the Gods? Pel didn't know if it was a cruel joke by the fates, or just his destiny. After all, wasn't there a prophecy that said Pel was Zeityl's destiny and his doom? Though it seemed to Pel that the reverse was true.

Zeityl.

He had fallen in love with a fucking God. With one of the murderers of his father.

"We don't know where he is," Pel said finally, that strange calm overtaking him once again. "He left, and all we know is that he said he was going to Nagir."

"That was a guise!" Utfer snapped. "Why would he go to Nagir? You must have done something to him?"

Pel crossed his arms across his chest, feigning a nonchalance he was far from feeling, even as worry knotted his insides. Where was Belthin? Or Zeityl. Whoever he was. If even the Gods couldn't find him, where could he be? What had he done?

"What could I have done to a God?" he asked. "Aren't you overestimating my abilities?"

The Gods looked at each other, perhaps realising the truth of his words. Pel had no idea how powerful Zeityl was, but he had a feeling that he was definitely more powerful than him.

"You're not fully human," one of the Gods said. "The cursed blood of an ancient race flows through your veins. You have inherited their magic and powers, and you are powerful, Pelthiel. Perhaps powerful enough to have harmed our brother."

"You're all insane!" Leithia snapped. "Honestly, we didn't even know who he was. Do you think we would have fucking risked our lives if we knew he was a God? Why would we harm him after saving his lives? Are you all usually this stupid, or are you making a special effort for us?"

One of the warriors of Nagir lifted their spear. "Watch your words, blasphemous human!"

"We're not afraid," Pel said drily. "If you're here to fight us, do it. Otherwise, get out. We don't know where Zeityl is, and as my sister said, we didn't even know who he was till you told us."

For the first time, doubt appeared on the faces of some of the Gods.

"You're lying!" Utfer said. "I'll kill you!"

"If you think I am so powerful that I could have harmed Zeityl, what chance do you think you could have?" Pel asked. "Like my sister said, are you making a special effort to be exceptionally stupid here?"

"Then where is he?" another God demanded. "If you didn't harm him, how is it that we can't sense him? How is it that we can't find him?"

"How is that our problem?" Leithia asked. "Are we responsible for your family problems now?"

Pel rather enjoyed the anger on the Gods' faces, but Utfer stepped forward again. "You are disrespecting the Gods!" he thundered. "Do you think you can get away with that?"

"You are the ones who came to our house and started flinging accusations," Pel said drily even as his heart raced. "Don't expect us to kneel down and bow."

"I will make you kneel!" Utfer snapped, and held out a hand.

Pel threw up a shield on instinct, enveloping both him and his sister. He felt Utfer's power buffeting the shield, but it held firm.

"You are powerful," Utfer said. "But are you more powerful than the Gods?"

This time, it wasn't just one God's power, it was all of theirs, and Pel's shield shattered, and he went to his knees as did Leithia. The next spell should have killed them, but another shield sprang up between them and the Gods.

"Stop this," a voice spoke, and Pel turned his head to see Belthin, or rather, Zeityl. There was no mistaking who he was now, and his face was stern as he looked at his siblings. "You shall not harm them."

"Zeityl," Utfer said, looking surprised and joyful. "Brother, you're safe!"

"You give the humans too much credit to think they could have harmed me," Zeityl said, his gaze trained on his siblings, and clear disdain in his words. "You even brought an army. What were you thinking?"

Utfer looked ashamed, but one of the other Gods stepped forward, looking angry. "What if they didn't harm you? They're still who they are, and we need to get rid of them."

"Hamithia," Zeityl said coldly. "Are you hard of hearing? I told you that you shouldn't harm them. They're no threat to us."

"Now, maybe not, but what about the future?" Hamithia pressed.

"Then we shall deal with it then," Zeityl said. "For now, we should leave."

Pel felt drained, but a part of him was relieved. Even if he lied, in the end, Zeityl spoke for them, and the Gods were going to leave. He and Leithia could go back to their lives. The Gods wouldn't defy Zeityl, would they?

"No!" Another God looked livid. "This is a trick! They bewitched you somehow! Otherwise, you wouldn't speak like this!"

"Ementiar!" Zeityl growled. "You know nothing! Leave now!"

"You won't fight us for two half humans!" Ementiar shouted. "This has to be something they did to you!"

Before Pel could react, a spell hit Zeityl's shield, and then another. Even Zeityl's powers couldn't deal with that, of all his siblings moving against him, and the shield cracked. Desperate, Pel tried to shore it up with his own power, with Leithia helping, but neither of them could do anything as the shield cracked.

Another spell hit Pel, who went to his knees, and he knew this was it. This was the end. But the next spell found Leithia who had jumped in front of him.

"No!" Pel whispered as she fell on the ground, eyes glazed, clouded, and lay unmoving.

He looked at the Gods, and suddenly, it was as if they were nothing, their powers nothing.

His shield sprang to life, and the spell he cast was so powerful it brought most of the Gods to their knees.

"Pelthiel! No!" Zeityl shouted, putting himself between him and the other Gods. "Please, Pelthiel, don't do this!"

"Get out of my way," Pel said. "I won't ask again."

"I can't let you harm my siblings."

"They killed mine," Pel said.

"Please, Pelthiel, you can't bring her back by harming them. Please!"

The Gods looked afraid, and Pel had no idea why, and he didn't care.

Zeityl moved, and the Gods all vanished.

"Kill him for us!" Utfer shouted and the armies of Nagir surged forward.

"Die!" Pel screamed, his rage boiling over in a wave of magic that shook the earth and ripped it apart. Fire and lightning struck the armies, the smell of charred flesh and screams of people filling the air.

"Pel!" the voice was Serityl's. "Bring her. Let me take you away. Leave them! They are not worth your life."

Pel picked up the still form of his sister and walked to the ocean, his magic still wreaking havoc behind him. He stepped on to the waves, and Serityl held him afloat.

"Take us away," he whispered, and she did.

Behind him, the land burned, and lightning still struck it.

# INTERLUDE I

When he woke, it was dark, but that could be because he was in a dark room. Next, it occurred to him that he was still alive. Someone had saved him.

*Why can't humans just let others die? Why do they have to go on saving them?*

Zeityl rose from the pallet on which he lay. The room was unfurnished and unadorned, and he knew without going outside that it was noon, and that he had been unconscious for a day and a half, and that he was on an island.

That was enough to cause the invisible bands around his heart to tighten again, leaving him breathless. He knew exactly where he was.

Why did humans extol love so much when it brought so much pain? It was almost physical, how it felt like there was something stuck in his heart, in his lungs, in his throat, something that hurt.

*I am not made for pain.*

No God was. They knew joy, and fun and laughter, and

how it was to look at humans from afar and feel contemptuous and to mock them. They knew cruelty and anger and hate. They didn't know love or compassion. More than anything, they weren't supposed to love humans. Or to fall in love with them.

He wasn't supposed to fall in love with a human. He wasn't supposed to get his heart broken.

His lungs seemed incapable of taking in air and he stumbled out into the sunshine, gasping for breath. For a moment, he was blinded by the brightness, just as a human would have been. His eyes caught sight of a man standing at the edge of a cliff, looking down into the ocean. His rescuer, apparently. Zeityl's eyes focussed, and he stared, his heart suddenly squeezing painfully.

The figure standing still was so familiar to him, from the hair beginning to grey to the powerful frame and the worn clothes. He tried to speak, to call him by name, but all he could manage was a sound that even to his ears was more of a strangled sob than anything.

The man turned around and the black eyes that meet his were guarded.

"You saved my life," Zeityl finally managed to croak, an echo of words he had spoken so long ago.

Pelthiel's expression didn't change and Zeityl didn't like the silence, didn't like it that Pelthiel was so quiet.

"I didn't realise you were trying to kill yourself," Pelthiel spoke, the exact same words he had spoken to him that first time except it was all wrong, the tone, the expression on his face, the grey in his hair.

Pelthiel was too young for the grey, to look so bleak, to look so empty.

*I did this, me and my siblings.*

There was no smile on Pelthiel's face, no playful smirk, no

teasing note in his voice, and Zeityl was suddenly tired, so very tired of all this. He didn't want to be saved, he didn't want the pain, and he didn't want to look at Pelthiel and know that he had caused this, that he was responsible for that cold look.

"I was," he said when the weight of the silence was too heavy and Pelthiel moved, coming closer to him.

Zeityl stood still, not moving, till Pelthiel was close enough for them to be sharing air. Pelthiel lifted his hands and cupped his face, the gesture so familiar and intimate, evoking memories of the countless number of times he had done it before. Zeityl wanted to close his eyes so he wouldn't need to see how Pelthiel now looked at him as if he were a stranger, as if he hated him.

"Why?" Pelthiel asked, his voice so expressionless.

Zeityl stared at him, not understanding for a moment what Pelthiel was asking. Was he asking him why he was trying to kill himself or why he lied and pretended and destroyed everything between them? He settled for the former because even he was not certain how to answer if it was the latter.

"Because I lost you," he said, the pain in his chest almost unbearable now.

The hands dropped away and Pelthiel took a step back, his expression clouding. Zeityl wanted to cry but he would not do that, not now, not when Pelthiel was still looking at him, anger and sadness and emotions Zeityl couldn't even put a name to swirling in his eyes.

"You did," Pelthiel agreed, his voice quiet and Zeityl turned away, back into the darkness of the hut. It felt as if something was ripping him open from the inside.

"Why do you hate me so much?" Pelthiel asked from behind him and Zeityl stilled. "You and your siblings," Pelthiel continued. "Why do you perceive me as a threat?"

Zeityl wished he had a satisfactory answer. He could reply. Tell him they didn't know him, that they didn't know how to feel about his power, his magic; that they didn't know anything about people, or anyone except themselves; that they- he rather, didn't know what it felt to love, to fall in love.

But he remained silent. Pelthiel had told him he had lost him. What was the point in explaining anything now? Besides, no explanation would bring Leithia back.

"I'm going back," he said, turning to look at Pelthiel one last time. "To my siblings."

Pelthiel nodded as if it was no more than he had expected. "I won't be here when you return,"

Zeityl supposed he deserved that. Pelthiel thought he was going to his brothers for backup, to fight him. Let him think that. It was no less than he deserved.

"Would you really have drowned if I hadn't saved you?" Pelthiel asked.

It was not an unexpected question, but it still took Zeityl by surprise.

"Yes," he nodded. "This ocean... it is an enemy to us."

It wouldn't have killed him, but would have tormented him for all eternity.

"You're Gods," Pelthiel said. "And you were the ones that bound her... why can't you control her?"

"She's older than us," Zeityl said. "And in her element, she's more powerful than any of us. If we step into it, she will try to kill us."

*Or capture us.* That last remained unspoken.

"And yet you braved it twice," Pelthiel mused aloud. "We should have let you drown that first time. Leit had saved you, and yet..."

"Pelthiel..."

"I know you tried to help, but you could have helped more by staying to explain the truth to me instead of having your angry siblings land on my doorstep."

Zeityl swallowed. What could he say? Pelthiel was right. Zeityl had been too much of a coward, even now, when was looking for death, or at least the oblivion that Serityl could have given him, if she was merciful. How had Pelthiel even wrested him from her grasp, anyway?

"I need to go," he said finally.

"Of course," Pelthiel agreed, an odd note in his voice.

Zeityl looked at his face once more, fighting his desire to gather the other man in his arms and kiss him. Hadn't he lost all those rights?

If only he could turn back time! Zeityl would go back and would tell Pelthiel the truth. He should have trusted Pelthiel, and he shouldn't have allowed his siblings to try to hurt Pelthiel. He should have saved Leithia. It was too late now, and there was no turning the clock back. Zeityl pulled himself together.

"Goodbye," he said, and it sounded final.

# SIXTEEN

Heldith woke up with a scream dying in his throat. He stared around in some confusion before it struck him that he was in the room that he shared with his friends. It was still dark outside, the stars visible through the window. He heaved a sigh and looked at the others. Everyone was asleep. Did they have nightmares? He had never seen any sign of it, but then, none of them, not even Kiriel, had ever asked him about his, so it was possible he was missing theirs the same way they were missing his.

Heldith sat up on his bed. He couldn't remember what he had dreamt, only that it wrenched his heart and had caused his whole being to clench in fear and anguish. Why couldn't he remember? He got up and walked to the window. Perhaps he should be grateful he was still alive and able to see the sky and the stars. He leaned forward till his forehead was touching the pane. It was made of glass and was cold on his skin, which had been burning hot. How did he not notice it before?

There was movement outside the window, on the beach,

and his eyes could make out the robed figure of the man who had imprisoned him. Pelthiel. Did he suffer from sleepless nights then? It wouldn't be a surprise. The man was, after all, evil, the author of so much death and destruction that the Gods themselves had to choose champions to end him.

He sighed, feeling despondent. Chosen of the Gods! How proud he had been then, and just look at him now! How easily he had been beaten! All his strength, his skills and his magic not availing him in the slightest. His opponent was just too good. What was so incomprehensible was that instead of killing him, Pelthiel had chosen to keep him a prisoner on this island.

He turned from the window and went back to bed, sitting down on it and gazing at the three other beds in the room. Once every three years, the Gods chose a champion, and these people in here had all been chosen the same way he had been and had been defeated and imprisoned. But were they really prisoners? They couldn't leave the island, but within it, they were free to roam wherever they wanted, free to carry their weapons, practice their magic. Only, they couldn't go home, and there was no chance, no hope of anyone finding them. Had it not been for the special compass that the Gods themselves had given him, none of them would have been able to find their way here. The magic that cloaked this island, that protected it, was so powerful that even the Gods couldn't penetrate it.

Sivreth believed that the Gods had misled them and had used them. How could they have expected any of them to beat a foe they themselves could not? Besides, if Pelthiel was as bad as he was said to be, why didn't he kill them? But as Kiriel had pointed out, what about Nagir? The entire city had been levelled, and every last person slaughtered by Pelthiel. Also, if he wasn't so bad, why didn't he let them go? Why hold them here?

"He has some nefarious plan in mind," he had said darkly.

91

Amerla had stayed away from these discussions, but perhaps it was not to be wondered at. She had been here the longest, and she had left a new bride behind when she had come. It was possible that her wife had remarried now. It had been nine years, after all.

"Also," Kiriel had added, lowering his voice, "what about all the champions before Amerla? Remember the Gods said this had been going on for almost twenty years? Ever since Nagir and its people were brutally murdered? So where are they all? I tell you, he has some plan in mind for us!"

*Perhaps he is waiting to sacrifice us all to some dark powers at a propitious time. Perhaps that is why he is so powerful.*

Except, wasn't it Utfer who demanded human sacrifices, and wasn't it the people of Nagir who had indulged in the practice? From all accounts, they had been a nasty bunch, but for all that, did they deserve to be exterminated? What gave anyone the right to decide something like that? Overnight, Utfer had lost all his followers, which had resulted in his powers dwindling to almost nothing.

*Our faith is what keeps them strong and powerful.*

Why didn't it make him feel powerful? He sighed again before getting up and going to the window for the second time that night. Pelthiel was still there, his dark robes barely visible, but the hood was down and the white of his hair was easily seen. It was strange he should have such white hair. He was, what, thirty-seven? Thirty-eight? He was young anyway and had a face that was still unlined. Yet, his hair was completely white.

Heldith frowned again. This man had been only as old as him or slightly younger when he had destroyed Nagir and its inhabitants. What power he must have had even then! What evil took hold of his mind that he should have done something like

92

that? Did he regret it? Despite their freedom on the island, it was rarely they saw its master and even rarer that they spoke to him. It was a barrier between them, the memory of the fact that they had come here to kill him and had failed quite miserably.

Heldith turned from the window again and walked towards the door, after another fleeting glance towards the sleeping figures, He opened the door noiselessly and slipped outside, closing it quietly behind him. He made his way to the door that led outside and opened it. The cool breeze outside caused goosebumps to rise on his skin almost immediately and he walked towards the beach. The ocean was quiet this night, which was why he could hear the words so clearly.

"They're so young, Leithia," Pelthiel was murmuring softly, "How could they have been so evil as to send them after me? They're children. Did they really think they would defeat me?"

Heldith swallowed hard, before taking a couple of steps and clearing his throat loudly. Pelthiel didn't turn around, and Heldith walked till they were standing abreast.

"You couldn't sleep, either?" he asked.

"I rarely sleep," Pelthiel answered. "What about you?"

"Nightmares," Heldith muttered. "Strange thing is I can never remember them."

Silence fell.

"Consider yourself fortunate that you can't remember your nightmares," Pelthiel said, turning to look at Heldith.

Heldith swallowed hard, mesmerised by the intense gaze.

# SEVENTEEN

P el rarely interacted with his unwilling prisoners, and none of them had ever shown any signs of wanting to talk to him either. After all, they had come to kill him, and though he had defeated them, he had spared their lives. And then had refused to let them leave. How was one to find words to bridge all that?

Perhaps that was why he was surprised to see Heldith, of all people, approach him. Though Pel had no idea what it was Heldith saw in his sleep, he could guess.

"It is cold," he said, turning away. "You should go inside."

"So should you," Heldith said quietly, voice low, and yet clear enough to Pel, even over Serityl's song.

"I don't feel cold," Pel said dismissively. He could walk away, go back to his room, or just transport himself to the other side of the island.

And yet, Pel did nothing, staying where he was, allowing the silence to envelope him like a cloak, letting the comfort that another's human's presence brought, soothe some of the ache of loneliness that filled his days.

He could tell them why he didn't let them leave, but he doubted if they would believe him. If he hadn't ventured beyond this island all those years ago, he wouldn't have known either. The only way to convince them would be to take them away, and Pel didn't want to expose these children to danger.

They talked about him amongst themselves, and he could guess it was nothing good. It couldn't be. They had come here to kill him, after all.

"Why did you believe the Gods?" Pel asked, shattering the silence into shards.

"Nagir," Heldith said briefly.

Nagir. That day, when he had walked away, his wrath had rained lightning and fire not just on the people who had invaded his island, but their city as well, killing everyone there, every man, woman, child and animal. No one was spared, because it was not Pel's conscious will, but his fury, his anguish that had caused him to lose control over everything.

Regret was just one other companion that resided in his breast next to the empty space that once held his heart. Since losing Leithia, and after Zeityl's final act, Pel's heart had been dead. That he lived, breathed, and kept to a routine didn't mean anything. Existence and life were not the same, after all.

When the first of these children had come, Pel had been vaguely annoyed. He had speedily defeated and sent them on their way. But by now, he was used to this as well. The way a new person would come every three years to challenge him. He had let go of them at first before he went to the world outside and learned the truth. Since then, he had been keeping the ones that came here.

And yet, here was this boy, Heldith, who—

It was painful to look at him, and see traces of a face he had thought he had forgotten. Belthin might have been a disguise, a person who had never existed, but Heldith was real, and the similarities were striking. Almost frightening.

"Nagir," Pel said quietly.

"Why did you do that?" Heldith asked.

"What does it matter to you?" Pel asked. "You weren't even born back then."

"That doesn't mean I can't care," Heldith said.

"Keep on caring then," Pel said, but he still made no attempt to leave. "I'm not going to defend myself to someone who has already made up their mind."

"How do you know that?" Heldith asked. "I am asking, aren't I?"

Pel stared at him, turning his face away almost immediately. "You came here at the behest of the Gods to kill me. Am I so wrong in assuming that you had already formed your own judgement on me?"

"I... that was... the Gods... how can you blame the Gods?"

"I thought I was asking you," Pel said. "The so called chosen of the Gods. Should have known you were incapable of thinking for yourself."

This time, he did leave, transporting himself to the other side of the island, where he sat on one of the rocks, and let Serityl's waves lap at his feet, and the bottom of his pants.

*You're troubled, young one.*

"I miss her so much, Serityl," Pel whispered. "Do you think I will ever see her again?"

Serityl made no answer, which was an answer in itself. Pel had never heard of a soul reincarnating. All souls returned to the void and merged with it. Any new soul formed from it would be a completely different one.

But then there was Heldith who looked so similar to Belthin and whose soul bore a striking resemblance to Zeityl's.

"Is he still there?" he asked.

Serityl grew agitated. *He's asleep, always asleep. I offered to set him free once, and he refused... he says he can protect you better like this.*

*I don't need his protection. I need him.*

Pel didn't speak the words. There was no need to. It would make no difference in the end. No matter what Serityl said, Zeityl couldn't return, not as he had been. His soul was shattered when he had used his own magic to destroy himself in the ocean after Pel had left him. Serityl had imprisoned what was left of him, but even if she changed his mind, it was impossible for him to return. All he could do was dissipate, and Pel couldn't blame him for not doing that.

*But why did you have to leave? Why did you have to do it?*

There would be no answers, ever. It wasn't even that Pel had forgiven Zeityl for his betrayal, for his deception. He just missed him. Just as he missed his sister. It was a different kind of missing, but no less real.

Pel sighed. It was no use either way. Just as he would never see Leithia again, he would never see Zeityl either. Heldith now... if Serityl hadn't confirmed that Zeityl was still there, he would have thought he was Zeityl reborn. But then, Zeityl was a God, and his power was not mere magic. Was it so unlikely that a part of him had been reborn as Heldith even as the rest of him slept?

He wished there was a way for him to be certain.

"You told me about Heldith," he said aloud. "Why?"

*They're one, and yet not.*

*That's as clear as mud.*

*Heldith is not the one you loved, but he is also him. Your destiny, not your doom, as you are his.*

*I thought I was Zeityl's destiny and his doom.*

At least he now knew what that meant. If they had never met, neither Leithia nor Zeityl would be gone now.

*Heldith and you are also each other's destiny, but not doom.*

Pel scoffed. *He's a kid.*

*He won't be forever.*

*And I will always be old enough to be his father. This is ridiculous.*

Serityl made no answer.

# EIGHTEEN

The days were monotonous, but not the same. It was hard to tell the passage of time on the island and Heldith often wondered how anyone kept track of it.

"Have you talked to him?" he asked Amerla, curious.

There was a time when she and Pelthiel had been the only ones on the island, after all. How did she manage by herself? He would have gone mad with no one to talk to. He tried to push away the fact that he wished to talk to Pelthiel, that he felt drawn to him, despite everything he believed about him.

"Not much," she said after a moment. "What do you say to someone whom you came to kill and who spared your life after that? Sorry? Why did you do it? Let me go home?" She sighed and brushed her hand across her closely cropped black hair. "I was wounded quite severely in my battle with him. I thought I would die, and he... he nursed me back to health." She pulled up her tunic to reveal the large scar that ran the length of her torso across her back and snaking around her body. Heldith heard both Sivreth and Kiriel gasp. She dropped the tunic and

STOLEN FROM A DREAM

continued. "He could have just let me die, but he didn't. He didn't just spare my life, he *saved* it. After that, how can I even look him in the face with the knowledge that I came here, to his home, his island of isolation, to *kill* him? And for what? Because some Gods said he was evil and that they had chosen me? If I were chosen, he shouldn't have been able to defeat me."

That was the most emotion he had ever heard in her voice. That was the most words she had ever spoken to them ever. At least since he came here. Guilt? Grief? It was all there.

"Like I always said, he's not evil," Sivreth said. "An evil man wouldn't have let us live, let alone gone to all that trouble to save our lives. Come on! It's not that hard to work it out."

"Then why doesn't he let us go?" Kiriel asked. "Why did he destroy Nagir?"

"A city full of Utfer fanatics, involved in human sacrifice?" Sivreth scoffed. "Not a loss by any stretch."

"What gave him the right to decide that?" Heldith asked. "The King made the sacrifices voluntary, which means that they weren't forcing anyone."

"You bet they found ways around that," Sivreth said.

"Even if it were so, what gave him the right to destroy them?" Heldith repeated. "Man cannot play God like that."

"The Gods have been doing a great job, haven't they?" Amerla muttered, bitterness evident in her words.

"So you agree with Sivreth?" Kiriel asked. "That this man is good?"

"I don't know," Amerla muttered. "I'm torn. I... He was.... He was so kind, so caring when he took care of me. But then he chose not to let me go, and that makes me wish sometimes that he had killed me outright instead because to live like this..."

Heldith understood. Kiriel sat down on a stump.

"I get you," he said. "I've a girl back home, too. We

100

weren't promised, but... it was an understood thing."

Sivreth shrugged. "Frankly, I'm not too upset he didn't let me go. My parents were... unkind is the kindest thing I can say about them. If not for my brother, I would be happy to stay here forever."

"I'm sorry," Heldith said. "But the thing is Sivreth, just because you don't want to go home and he kept you here doesn't mean he's a good man. I mean, why would the Gods choose to destroy him if he were good?"

"Because they're a bunch of jealous, petty, vengeful fools?" Sivreth offered.

"That won't do," Kiriel said. "He did destroy Nagir and killed thousands. There's no way you can get around that. He destroyed Utfer's power. Why wouldn't the Gods want him gone after that?"

"They said it wasn't the worst thing he did," Heldith said, remembering his vision. "They said it was so heinous they couldn't even speak of it."

It had made such an impression on him at that time. The words, and the heaviness of the tone and the voice.

"Eyewash!" Sivreth snorted.

"If the Gods are so perfect," Amerla interrupted whatever reply Kiriel was about to make. "How did we lose? They chose us. Doesn't that mean we should have won?"

"His power," Kiriel muttered, looking away, towards the outer edge of the cliff they were on, where the ocean glittered. "How can we ever have hoped to win against it?"

"The Gods are more powerful, aren't they?" Sivreth asked. "Then why didn't they just come here and destroy him? Why send us? As Kiriel said, he's far too powerful for us. Didn't they know that?"

"Look, maybe the Gods aren't everything we believed

them to be," Heldith said, leaning against a withered tree. "They may not be infallible or all powerful, but that doesn't make *him* good."

Uncomfortably, the words he had heard Pelthiel speak the previous night intruded into his mind. He had sounded as if he was angry at the Gods for sending them to him. His words, "*they're just children*," kept repeating in his mind. Was that how Pelthiel saw them? Was that why he had kept them alive? There were a lot of things he wanted to know, but how was he going to find out?

"Why don't we go and ask him?" he asked abruptly.

"Ask him what?" Amerla asked.

"Why he didn't kill us, why he isn't letting us go home, why he destroyed Nagir... what was the unspeakable thing he did?"

Even Sivreth looked uncomfortable. "Do you think he'll tell us?" he asked.

"Maybe not about Nagir, or whatever the Gods claim he did," Amerla said. "But... the other... it concerns us directly... he can't refuse to answer us, can he?"

"Of course he can, but even if he doesn't, how do we know he'll tell us the truth?" Kiriel said.

"A truth spell," Heldith said.

"I don't think any of us can bind him with a truth spell unless he lets us," Kiriel objected again.

"We can take him by surprise," Sivreth said. "We would need to be bound to the spell as well, is all."

"A five-way bond," Kiriel muttered, picking up a stick and starting to break it into five before arranging the pieces on the ground. "Like this?"

"That won't work," Heldith said. "He's the most powerful. He needs to be the locus."

"True," Kiriel muttered. "All right."

He rearranged the sticks with one in the centre and the other four in the corners of an invisible square. "But what good would this do? Even if we learn he's going to sacrifice us to the ocean on the next full moon, there isn't anything we can do, is there?"

"Look," Heldith said. "Individually none of us are a match for him, and perhaps together also, we're not, but so far we've not considered escaping or seeking help or anything because we've got used to this. If we know he's planning something bad, then we can take risks we aren't willing to now."

From the arrested looks on their faces, he knew he had them convinced. It was obvious none of them had ever thought of it that way. They all knew how dangerous it was to try to escape. But if they all put their powers together, theoretically, at least one or two of them could. The risk hadn't seemed worth it, but if Pelthiel was planning to kill them anyway, the risk was acceptable. Heldith was ready to give his life to help the others escape.

"We may not even need to," Sivreth said, sounding troubled. "He may have nothing bad in mind."

"We'll know soon," Heldith said, silencing the voice inside him that told him this was a bad idea and that he was going to regret it.

*Why should I regret it?*

Except there was a lump of uncertainty in his mind. But he had to know one way or another what was the fate in store for him and his friends. Heldith couldn't live like this. He would grow insane. He missed his family, his parents, and their love, not to speak of his best friend. Ryr and he had known each other since they had been babies. It had been hard to come on this adventure alone.

Ryr had protested vehemently, stating that heroes need sidekicks, but the Gods had been specific. Heldith and only Heldith should go. He was glad he had listened. It wouldn't have done to trap Ryr here on this island as well. He would have got into all kinds of trouble and would have pestered Pelthiel with so many questions. But perhaps Pelthiel would have let them go to escape from Ryr. Or turned him into a statue. Anything was possible.

"So when do we do this?" Amerla asked, studying the diagram Kiriel had drawn on the grassy ground using magic.

"Tonight," Kiriel said. "After dinner. He won't be expecting anything."

"He never does," Heldith muttered.

Either Pelthiel was too trusting or too arrogant, but he didn't seem to anticipate they might band together against him. He was in for a surprise.

Heldith forcibly shut down the little voice in his head that warned him this was the worst idea ever.

# NINETEEN

"**B**etrayal comes naturally to you, doesn't it?" Pel asked, glaring at Heldith, the words slipping out before he could help it.

In retrospect, he should have seen it coming. He should have anticipated this. He knew that his guests, his prisoners, weren't happy to be held here, and he had known from the moment Heldith came that nothing was going to be the same. After Serityl's words, it had become a near certainty that he might find himself involved in another fight.

Heldith obviously didn't know the truth about himself, despite whatever nightmares he had. It wasn't strange that he couldn't remember them. What was strange was that the ones who had sent him here hadn't chosen to enlighten him, to remove whatever barrier was preventing him from realising the truth.

*Perhaps they don't know either.*

Blind as they were, it would be no surprise. None of that would save Pel from his present predicament, however. The truth spell had him as the locus with the four youngsters' magic bolstering it and binding all five of them together. They had planned it well. But why a truth spell? Why not try an attack spell or a killing spell?

"Why this one?" he asked, outwardly calm, though inwardly his insides were writhing in anxiety. "You could have attacked me, killed me even."

"Not without killing ourselves, too," Kiriel said. "This way, we all just have to tell the truth for a while."

Pel nodded. "True. Well, if we're going to exchange confidences, we might as well be civilised about it. No need to do this at the dinner table, is there?"

They had chosen their places at the table with care tonight. How did he not even notice it? No use going over that now. He had been complacent, expecting them to adapt to life here, and though he had sensed their discontent, he had hoped it would go away with time. It might have too, if Heldith had not come. The others had all but reconciled to their lot.

Pel held himself in control as he led them into the room where he spent most of his days. It had a window with a view of the ocean and the fire crackling in the hearth provided warmth as well as light. There were enough chairs in here and on one corner was the shelf containing his scrolls and books and on the other side of the room was the door leading to his workshop. He took a chair and waved the others to the remaining ones, and there were still two empty chairs. Sometimes Pel didn't know why he had made so many chairs, but it had been something to do in the earlier years when he had been alone and hurting, wanting to forget, wanting to do something.

That frenzy had faded now, and he was calmer. The grief would never fade, but he was past the point of self-destruction, or destroying the world.

"So," he said. "Ask. Obviously, there is something you're

eager to know or you wouldn't have gone to all this trouble."

He could guess what they wanted to know, but he was going to make them ask. He had to stay in control, make it seem as if he still had the upper hand. Keep them off balance. The four looked discomfited and looked at one another as if hesitant to open the conversation.

"I'll ask something then," he said. "Tell me why you did this now. What was the need?"

"Because we need to know what you plan to do with us," it was Kiriel who spoke, which wasn't a surprise. The young man had so much courage.

"I don't plan to do anything." Pel was amused, though he didn't show it. What did they think he was going to do to them?

"Except keep us here, your prisoners, for the rest of our lives," Heldith said.

Ah. There wasn't anything he could say about that. They were right, of course.

"Is that your plan?" Sivreth asked.

"To keep you here, yes," Pel said. In a way, the truth spell was a good thing. It meant he could finally tell them the truths he had locked in his chest for fear they wouldn't believe him if he revealed them.

"Why wouldn't you let us go?" Heldith asked at the same time as Amerla asked, "Why didn't you kill us?"

Neither question was very easy to answer. But he could tell them, and they would believe him because of the truth spell, but the answers might not be what they expected, and it wasn't easy for him to say the words.

"Which do you want answered first?" he asked.

"Why did you spare us?" Sivreth asked.

"What else was there to do?" he asked. "You were here and I'm not a cold-blooded murderer, whatever you've been led to believe."

Kiriel opened his mouth, a furious expression on his face, but Heldith interrupted whatever he was going to ask. "Why didn't you let us go, then? Why keep us here?"

"As I said," he said. "I'm not a cold-blooded murderer."

"What's that supposed to mean?" Kiriel asked.

"Do you know what happened to those who came here before you?" Pel asked. "I let them go. Do you know what happened to them?"

"What happened to them?" Heldith asked.

"They were all killed," Pel said, feeling his shoulders slump. It was times like these that he felt as if he was way older than his forty years. "The Gods sent visions to the priests of their hometowns and villages. They failed in their mission and were to be sacrificed to Utfer."

"No," Kiriel said. "You're lying!"

He was extremely pale and so were the rest of them. Pel sighed as he said, "You cast the spell. You know I'm telling the truth. You just don't want to believe that the Gods you follow blindly don't have any more care for you than they do for any inanimate weapon they may choose to you."

"You're saying they would have caused us to be killed if you let us go," Heldith said.

Pel nodded.

"But you must have let go how many people before us? Three? Four? Why? If you knew?" Amerla's voice was shaking.

"I didn't," Pel couldn't help the bitterness that crept into his voice. "I thought they were home and safe. I keep to myself, I never leave here, but..." He swallowed, looking out the window, though the glass reflected only his own face, pale and tired. "I had to leave once... the why isn't important." He avoided looking at Heldith as he spoke. "But I thought I would check in on all the champions who had come after me..."

"And you found out they'd all been sacrificed to Utfer," Kiriel said, his whole body trembling.

"The price of their failure," Pel said quietly. "The next year, you came, Amerla, and I knew once I had saved you that I couldn't send you back, knowing what awaited you."

"You could have told us," Sivreth said.

Pel snorted. "And you would have believed me?"

"We wouldn't have," Kiriel muttered. "This is... I don't know what to say, what to think."

"Remove the spell," Pel said quietly. "You have your answers."

The four stood forming the four corners of an unseen square with him in the middle. They made identical motions and Pel felt the spell release him from its grip. He sagged, exhaustion as well as relief coursing through him.

"Thank you," he said. "Go to bed. Please."

They left silently, except Heldith, who lingered, his eyes on Pel.

"What did you mean?" he asked. "When you said betrayal comes naturally to me?"

He looked troubled, and Pel shrugged. "Nothing,"

"You're lying," Heldith said quietly.

Pel didn't answer. Heldith's eyes searched his face before he sighed and turned to go.

"Good night, Pelthiel."

Again, Pel made no reply. What was there to say, anyway? The truth about Heldith was even wilder than the truth about why he held them here.

# TWENTY

Heldith was drowning; the ocean had him in her grip. He choked and struggled, trying to break her hold, but she held on fast. He could hear her laughter as she whispered, "Finally, I'll have my revenge!"

Heldith had no doubt about that, though why she was talking of revenge was something he didn't know. His lungs burned and he could feel the darkness waiting at the edge of his consciousness, waiting to take him. His struggles were growing feebler. It felt as if his limbs were made of stone. He tried to beg her to release him, to let him live, but the words wouldn't make their way out.

A hand caught him. A human hand, that slowly but inexorably, drew him upwards towards the surface till finally his head broke it. Heldith heaved in lungfuls of air, coughing and choking and shaking. He turned to look at his rescuer and saw Pelthiel whose face was stern and different. He looked younger, his hair was close cropped and his curls lay like a cap framing his face. There were grey and white streaks in his hair, and his face was younger too.

"Zeityl," Pelthiel said.

Heldith woke, his heart hammering. The nightmare still clung to him and he looked around wildly, expecting to see water and slumped back, relieved, when he saw he was still on his bed. It had been so vivid. He could still feel the salty taste of the water in his mouth and he was taking in breaths, as if he had been drowning a moment ago. Why did he have a dream about drowning and about Pelthiel? It made no sense. Heldith was a strong swimmer and had always been. Ryr used to call him half a fish. Why should he ever have a dream about drowning? And why was it about Pelthiel? Who was Zeityl?

It took him a moment longer to realize that he had, for the first time in his life, remembered a nightmare. It made him sit up, heart racing. For a moment, he was so stunned by the realisation that all thoughts of the nightmare were driven from his mind. He remembered nights of waking in blind panic, taking in lungfuls of air and trying to calm himself down. He remembered times when he had woken up in tears, his heart wrenched in grief and not remembering why. But today, somehow, he had remembered. Had he been dreaming of drowning all this time? *Have I been dreaming of Pelthiel all this time?* Was that why he felt so drawn to the man?

But Pelthiel had called him Zeityl in the dream. Who was that? Why did the name sound so familiar, even though he was certain he had never heard it before? Perhaps he had heard it in the nightmares that he could not remember.

Hldith got out of the bed and tiptoed to the door. He had to see Pelthiel, talk to him. He stopped just outside the room where they slept. Where did Pelthiel sleep anyway? The house was large, and he had never once explored it, confining himself to the room where they slept and the kitchen and dining areas. The first time he had seen anything other than that was when Pelthiel had taken him to his study. Library. Whatever.

That was the only room he knew, but Pelthiel wouldn't be there, would he? He was likely to be asleep, and was it a good idea to wake a powerful sorcerer at this time? But what if he wasn't asleep? He had said he didn't sleep much.

Even without his volition, his feet had been carrying him forward, towards the room where Pelthiel had talked to them the night that had changed them forever. Somehow, the knowledge that they could never go back, of the fate that awaited them if they did, had caused a despondence in them that wasn't easy to shake off. For the last one week, they had either stayed in the room or went out to the cliff and had sat at their usual place, not saying anything, but gazing out into the ocean. None of them knew what to say or think. It would have been comfortable if they could accuse Pelthiel of lying, but there was the truth spell.

Heldith stopped in front of the door to the room. The door was ajar, and he saw light flickering within. He pushed it open slightly. Pelthiel was sitting by the fire, reading something, and he lifted his face from the book as Heldith entered. His face was shadowed in part, and Heldith wished he could see his eyes.

"What is it?" Pelthiel asked.

"Who is Zeityl?"

It hadn't been what he had meant to ask, but it slipped out of him. Pelthiel's gaze became fixed and there was a flash of what seemed like pain across his features. He turned his head away from Heldith and looked at the fire.

"Where did you hear that name?"

"Who is he?"

Pelthiel made no answer, and Heldith huffed in annoyance as he moved into the room, closing the door behind him. He walked to where Pelthiel was sitting, his gaze seemingly riveted on the crackling flames, and pulled a chair next to him and sat down.

"I had a nightmare," he said. "I was drowning, or rather the ocean was trying to drown me. You saved me; you were younger, and you called me Zeityl."

"How do you expect me to know what a name in your dream means?" Pelthiel asked, not looking at him. "Just because I was in your dream doesn't mean I know anything about it."

It was logical, reasonable, and yet, Heldith was certain it was a lie. Accusing Pelthiel of it was not going to do any good, however. He possessed no skills to make this man tell him the truth. He could try a truth spell, but it was likely Pelthiel would swat it aside. After the last time, none of the others might be eager to try another one.

"Will you ever tell me the truth?" he asked at last.

Pelthiel turned to look at him. "Why do you assume I'm lying?"

"I know," he said quietly. "I know you know who Zeityl is, and I think you know about my nightmares... this is the first one I had ever remembered, but I'm sure I've been having this same dream for all my life. Why would I even dream of you when I didn't know you?"

"Do you expect me to know the answer to that?" Pelthiel asked quietly.

Heldith was the one who turned his face away. He felt a despair that had nothing to do with his situation.

"I'm not a dream interpreter," Pelthiel said quietly.

"I'm sorry I bothered you," Heldith said quietly, his despair growing.

Pelthiel sighed. "Zeityl was a God," he said after a moment.

Heldith looked at him, astonished. "A God? I've never

113

heard of a God named Zeityl."

"That's because he's dead," Pelthiel said. "He died around twenty years back."

"Around the time you destroyed Nagir?" Heldith asked.

Pelthiel looked at the fire again.

"Yes," he said, his voice sounding strange. "Around that time. After Nagir was destroyed."

"Did you know him? Did he talk to you in dreams or visions?"

Pelthiel shook his head. "I thought I knew him, but no. He never talked to me in dreams or visions."

"How did he die?"

"I do not know," Pelthiel said. "All I know is that the Gods have blamed me for his death. That is why I had to hide myself away, but it does seem as if they'll never let me be."

Heldith had a feeling there was more to the tale, but he was also certain he was not going to learn anything more tonight. But at least now he knew what the heinous act that the Gods wouldn't even speak of was. Pelthiel sounded as if he had nothing to do with Zeityl's death, but the Gods obviously thought different. Why, though? Who was right? Heldith didn't know who to trust anymore.

# TWENTY ONE

Pel wandered the island, his feet carrying him without any input from his brain. It was as if he just wanted to escape, go as far away from the house as possible. As far away from Heldith, and the truth that he had almost let slip last night, away from the haunted eyes of the youth, so similar to the eyes that still haunted his dreams.

But Zeityl was gone, and Heldith was not him, no matter that he was still a part of Zeityl. It was that part that bothered Pel. Because there was more to Heldith than just Zeityl, but somehow that part of Zeityl seemed to be all he could see, and that upset him. He didn't want to look at Heldith and see Zeityl, but after what he had done, what they had done, it was all Pel could focus on.

In the end, Heldith had proved as deceptive as Zeityl. In the end, Pel couldn't trust any of the people on this island though he had saved them. He didn't know whose idea the truth spell was, whose idea it was to trap him, to use his own power against him, but did that matter? All the others had gone along with it, none had hesitated. In the end, Pel's choice, his free will hadn't mattered to any of them.

Perhaps he should just let them go free. Back to wherever they came from, to face whatever consequences of failure awaited them. But no matter how much he might resent the present situation, and the people on his island, Pel wasn't as heartless as to send them to their deaths.

He wished he had another option. He could ask Serityl to take him away, but then he'd lose the protection this island provided. Pel would be throwing away Zeityl's sacrifice. No matter how angry he was at Zeityl, and how much it hurt, he still appreciated that the God wanted to protect him, had given up his life to do it.

*I only ever wanted to share your life, Zeityl. Why did you have to burden me like this?*

But what was done was done, and couldn't be undone. For Zeityl's sake, if nothing else, he had to stay here.

But any other place was risky for the youngsters as well. Pel hadn't saved them, hadn't spent time and effort on making them live, just for the Gods to kill them.

*They're unimportant,* Serityl's voice wafted over. *You can't always save everyone, Pelthiel.*

*It seems like I can't save anyone.*

*You care for these young people.*

*I do, no matter what they did, what they came for, I care. I've caused far too much destruction, far too much death already, Serityl. I don't wish to cause any more.*

*You are not responsible for their lives or choices. Pelthiel, you can only try your best.*

*I want to make amends for the deaths I caused, but I don't know how. Saving these lives is the least I can do.*

Serityl didn't argue anymore, and Pel was grateful. She had somehow grown more coherent and sane since Zeityl had shattered his soul and allowed her to take him. Sometimes, Pel wondered if he made it so when he made the choice to destroy himself. Just like the choice he had made to protect Pel.

*Thinking about it will get you nowhere, young one. He loved you, and he wanted to make amends too.*

"It's not the same," Pel muttered aloud.

*No, but what is? You're not living a life here. You're barely existing. This is not what he wanted for you.*

*He shouldn't have done what he did then. He should have stayed with me.*

Serityl was silent and Pel threw himself down on to the mossy ground, looking up at the sliver of sky visible through the treetops.

*I miss you, Leit. I wonder if I'll ever see you again.*

She was part of the endless nothing, and he would be there as well someday. But for now, he would stay here and do what he can to make amends for the terrible things he had done.

# TWENTY TWO

Heldith entered the small pool, feeling the water cool down his skin. He didn't come out here by himself very often, but the others preferred to bathe in the bathhouse near the house and Heldith had wanted a swim. The pool wasn't large enough for more than a few lengths, nor deep enough to drown in. Ever since his nightmare, he had been afraid to swim in the ocean.

He had nightmares again, but none he could recall except the drowning one. That one he had twice more. Every time he saw the ocean now, he could feel the salt in his tongue and the burning of his lungs, and the malevolence that had enveloped him. That was what frightened him the most. The sense of hatred he had felt emanating from the ocean, the inexorable determination to end him. Part of him mocked himself for being a fool, for being this affected by what was only a dream, but the other part warned him that it was real, that it had happened, that the ocean wouldn't spare him now that he had become aware.

Aware of what?

He huffed in frustration as he swam. His own mind

seemed to be playing with him. It was like there was something there, just beyond the edges of his conscious awareness, a knowledge of why these dreams, a memory of what they were, a recognition that knew both Pelthiel and Zeityl, but it eluded his grasp. It was as smoke in the wind, without form or substance, visible and yet out of his reach. Despite all evidence to the contrary, he couldn't shake off the feeling that Pelthiel knew what his own mind hid from him. The man would not tell him anything, though. That much had been made evident to him by their conversation the night he had woken from that nightmare.

How was he supposed to know if no one would tell him? Even a truth spell might not help. Truth spells could not compel people to speak, it only made it that what they spoke was the truth. Pelthiel had told them about the fate in store for him because he had wanted them to know, and he didn't have to fear that they would disbelieve him. The spell would not have loosened his tongue on anything he didn't want them to know.

He reached the other end of the pool and turned, and twisted, and was soon on his back, swimming with lazy strokes towards the other shore. The pool was ringed around with trees, but he could see the sky and the sun from here. The sun was shining directly on to him, its rays warming the water and causing rainbows in the droplets flung about by the movement of his body.

He would need to get out of the water and help Pelthiel with preparing food. They had always helped him with chores ever since they had realised that he never used magic for that. They were rather surprised that he didn't use magic, but it made sense. Pel's power was far too great, and would likely not be able to control the finesse needed for household tasks.

Pel?

Ever since they had learned the truth, there had been a

difference in how they acted around him. Despite how bitter and sad they were, they were not treating him with hostility now. Pelthiel still treated them the same way he had treated them always. He accepted their help and thanked them for it, but he made no attempts to be friendly or even to converse with them.

What was there to talk about anyway? Whatever secrets were buried in Pelthiel's heart, whatever there was about his past wasn't likely to be any more palatable than the truth that they had already wrenched out of him. Of course, it was a relief knowing that they were not going to be killed on the next full moon or whatever, but that didn't make it any easier to reconcile themselves to the prospect of staying here for the rest of their lives.

"Hey." The familiar voice startled him and he twisted around, treading water, his feet finding the bottom as he turned fully around to see Kiriel standing there.

"What the-" Heldith glared at Kiriel. "Did you have to sneak up like that?"

"Sorry," Kiriel said. "But you've been gone for hours, and we got a bit worried. Also, you missed lunch."

Hours? He opened his mouth to refute when he became aware that the sun was no longer visible above the pool and that the atmosphere had begun to darken. The skin on his body had become wrinkled, and he was shivering. He was also hungry. How did he not notice it before? He got out of the water, accepting the towel Kiriel held out and started to dry himself.

"You look troubled," Kiriel said as Heldith began to dress.

"I didn't notice how much time had passed," he said.

How had it happened? He could have sworn he had been in the water for a few minutes only.

"Well, our host said there was a storm coming, and it was

better to stay indoors for now. So, I thought I'd come looking for you."

"Thank you," Heldith said with real gratitude.

Being caught out here in a storm was not a prospect to be relished.

As they walked home, Heldith said, "Do you think he would tell us anything if we were to ask him? About Nagir I mean?"

"It's none of our fucking business, is it?"

"I know, I just... Kiriel, can I tell you something?"

Kiriel looked at him, not slacking his pace or stopping, but there was a great deal of shrewdness in his eyes. "Is this anything of a confidential nature?"

Was it? It could be said so, but honestly? He didn't care who found out. If he were back home, it would have been a different matter altogether, but not out here.

"Not really," he said. "I mean, yeah if we were back home, but not here."

"I know what you mean," Kiriel muttered. "So, what is it?"

Heldith wasn't sure what he wanted to say, but he found himself pouring it all out, his nightmares, his conversation with Pelthiel, the strange feeling he had that there was something buried in his own mind, and his newfound fear of the ocean. For some reason he didn't mention Zeityl. It wasn't deliberate, but still he found himself skirting over any mention of Zeityl or his name.

Kiriel heard him out in silence, saying at the end of it, "Why do you think Pelthiel knows anything? As he said, because he appears in your dreams doesn't mean he knows anything. Besides, have you considered that your dreams are just, dreams? Perhaps it is just your mind's symbolic representation of how he spared you instead of killing you?"

It was logical and reasonable and Heldith hated that explanation.

"I know that what I'm saying makes no sense," he sighed. "And I don't know, maybe you're right, except I just have this feeling that they are more. I know that's as stupid as the rest, but," he shrugged.

"Sivreth is an adept at dream interpretation," Kiriel said. "We can ask him, and if he thinks your feelings have any basis, we can ask Pelthiel. But if already refused to tell you, I don't know why he should tell any of us anything now."

"I know," he muttered. "But what else can we do if these dreams are more than dreams?"

Kiriel made no answer. The day darkened further and the wind picked up. They both increased their pace as a streak of lightning split the sky. Heldith was troubled more than he was ready to admit. If he was to seek help from Sivreth, he would need to tell him about Zeityl. He didn't know why that bothered him, but it did.

# TWENTY THREE

Pel woke with the sound of Leithia's voice still in his ears and the feel of the spray of ocean on his body. It had been just a dream. He wouldn't call it a nightmare. Not when he could see her, as real as she had been in life. The vividness of the dream, the clarity of his memory of that day astounded him.

That had been the day it had all started. The beginning of the end for them both. The day they had saved Belthin, no, Zeityl.

He sat up in his bed and stared out into the night, at the heavily falling rain and the lightning that flashed across the sky, and the crashes of thunder that were so loud he was surprised he had slept through it. Rain had clouded the glass of the windows that he couldn't see anything. Not that there was anything to see out there at this time.

He moved towards the windows, casting a spell to remove and repel the water from the glass panes so he could stare outside. It must have been the storm that forced that memory to the fore. He hadn't thought of that day in such a long time.

He sighed and was about to turn away when he became aware of the figure outside. He was almost invisible in his soaked clothes as he walked towards the ocean with purposeful steps, but Pel recognised Heldith. For a moment, his blood froze cold; the next, he was running towards the door and outside. Blind panic gripped him, even as he cursed himself.

He was a damn fool! Would he never learn? But he couldn't let Heldith drown. He was probably sleepwalking and in his current state, he was vulnerable. Serityl already knew him, and for all her words to Pel, he didn't think she would spare Heldith if she got her hands on him. Her hatred of the Gods ran deeper than any concern she might have for Pel.

Pel didn't want to think of that. He ignored the rain lashing him as he ran towards Heldith, hoping that he wouldn't be too late. He didn't even stop to think of his dream that seemed like a premonition now.

"Heldith!" he shouted as he ran. "Heldith, stop!"

Heldith didn't hear him, and Pel's magic reached out to create a barrier in front of the young man, but he walked through it as if it was nothing. No wonder, if he was Zeityl. Even if he was only a part of Zeityl, he probably had all of Zeityl's power.

Since the day of Leithia's death, Pel had known that had Zeityl chosen to stand with his siblings that day, he would have been dead as well. The Gods together were powerful, but Zeityl had been more powerful than all of the others combined, and even Pel was not a match for him.

Perhaps it was lucky that Heldith couldn't use that power except when he was asleep, or Pel would be dead now.

Cursing himself, he ran after Heldith, not daring to use any more magic in the blinding rain.

# TWENTY FOUR

The ocean was waiting for him and he was walking into it. It was familiar and comforting and held the answers he sought. He had heard her call, and he knew she would reveal all. He smiled as he approached her. This was where he belonged; this was what he deserved.

He paused, unsure, and in that instant, a hand closed over his arm, the grip vice-like, and Heldith woke with a start. Even through the pelting rain, he couldn't but recognise Pelthiel. He was bewildered. The last he remembered he had been on his bed, about to fall asleep, so what was he doing here by the ocean? Dread settled on his stomach, heavy as lead as he saw how near he was to the sea. Pelthiel had once again saved his life.

"What happened?" he asked, allowing himself to be pulled along.

"You were sleepwalking, right into the ocean," Pelthiel said.

"Yeah, I can see that," Heldith muttered.

That was not what he meant, but what was he expecting

Pelthiel to say? Once they were inside the house, Pelthiel said, "You should go and change. Come to the library afterwards. Let me see what I can do."

Heldith nodded, and trudged back to his room, water dripping off of him in rivulets. He entered the room just as a crash of thunder pealed and all three of his friends woke up startled.

"What-" Sivreth started

"Why are you wet?" Amerla asked.

Kiriel was just looking at him without a word.

"I sleepwalked straight into the ocean," Heldith said. "Pelthiel stopped me." he paused. "He wants to talk to me."

"We'll come with," Amerla said. "If he's trying to keep you safe, we too need to know how."

Heldith felt a surge of relief, though it was tinged with annoyance as well. He couldn't explain why. He was happy his friends would be with him. Somehow Pelthiel had looked intimidating.

*He can't blame me for sleepwalking, can he?*

Not that Pelthiel appeared to be blaming him. He had looked and sounded worried more than anything. Why? Heldith could understand why he had spared him, but why save his life now? Why attempt to protect him? Unbidden, his recurring nightmare came to his mind. Pelthiel saving him, calling him Zeityl.

Zeityl who had been a God and who was now dead.

Somehow, he had to know more about Zeityl. Heldith had a feeling that the answers he sought lay there. But there was a frustrating lack of information about the Gods. Most people didn't even know all their names. He knew about Utfer only because the God who visited his dreams had told him. Even their priests didn't know what their powers were. How was he supposed to get information on a dead God?

*Ementiar, if you're able to hear this, please answer me.*

He had no hopes; after all, he had prayed for days after his defeat and had received no response, but he didn't know what else he could do. Pelthiel was refusing any answers he might have, and he was not sure how much Sivreth would be able to help, especially since Heldith couldn't even remember his dreams.

He dried himself mechanically, slipping out of his drenched clothes and putting on dry ones. He could hear his friends getting up and moving about. Would Pelthiel be angry if they accompanied him? But why should he be? He hadn't said to come alone. Besides, it was not as if he had woken them. The thunder did that.

They went towards the library, and Heldith wasn't sure what to expect. He was nervous, though he didn't know why. He knocked at the door and entered at Pelthiel's quiet, "Come inside."

The room felt more welcoming than their host, though he was not showing any signs of hostility or even irritation. If Pelthiel was surprised to see them all, he didn't show it, gesturing for them to be seated. The fire was burning brightly, pervading the room with light and warmth. The sounds of the rain were muted, and the windows were closed and so were the curtains.

"I think it is time something is done about your dreams," Pelthiel said quietly once they were all seated.

"Agreed." Kiriel was the one who answered. "Do you know anything about them?"

Pelthiel shrugged. "Why would I?"

"If Heldith trusts me, I can read his dreams," Sivreth said.

"That's just the problem," Heldith said. "I don't remember them. Except one, that is."

"Tell us about that," Sivreth said. "Perhaps we can help

you."

"I can help with the ones you can't remember," Amerla said. "I can bring forth hidden memories."

"Are you sure you want to do this?" Pelthiel asked. "It can be overwhelming,"

Heldith had no doubt, but he nodded. "I need to know. Why was I out there? Why do I have this feeling that I would have died if you hadn't stopped me even though I was the best swimmer in my town? Why does the ocean frighten me now?"

"All right," Pelthiel said. "When do you want to do this? Tonight?"

"In the morning," Heldith said.

Somehow the night with the storm raging outside seemed like a bad time to delve into the secrets of his own mind.

"I will have wards set around the house," Pelthiel said. "They should prevent any more sleep walking excursions."

Heldith had a feeling Pelthiel wasn't happy about what had just happened. But why? Why would Pelthiel care so much, especially after what happened the other day? What was he hiding? Despite his curiosity, Heldith felt no regret for his decision. He had to know. His life depended on it. If Pelthiel didn't like it, that was not his problem.

*What if I learn something I don't want to?*

It didn't matter. Whatever happened, he had to know the truth. They left the room and made their way back to their room.

"Are you sure about this, Heldith?" Kiriel asked.

"I don't know," Heldith said. "But if I don't try and find out, next time I could die. I can't always be depending on someone else coming to the rescue."

"All right. Go to bed then, and hopefully, you won't have any more nightmares tonight," Amerla said bracingly.

Heldith had no such hopes, but he nodded.

As soon as he closed his eyes, the vision swept over him.

*Heldith, I heard your prayer.*

*Ementiar?*

*Yes, my child. Is the criminal dead?*

*No, as you should know. He's much more powerful than I am.*

*I'm grieved to know he still lives. Where are you, child?*

*Don't know. Do you know who Zeityl is?*

Ementiar's calm facade cracked. The look of anguish on his face startled Heldith. How could a God be capable of pain like this? This grief?

*How do you know that name?* The question was asked in a whisper.

*I've been dreaming about him.* Not a complete lie.

*I thought... he killed him. Pelthiel. He killed Zeityl. He was our brother and that evil sorcerer killed him. That is why he must die. That is why we will never rest till he is dead!*

Heldith opened his eyes, his breath coming in gasps. He stared at the darkness, and remembered his dream, Pelthiel calling him Zeityl.

Why did he feel as if Ementiar was lying to him?

It was a blasphemous thought. Why would a God lie to him? What had he to gain? Heldith wished he had asked Ementiar about what Pel had said, about the truth of what had happened to the other heroes who had come here and who had been set free by Pel.

Pel had told him that the Gods believed he had killed Zeityl, but hadn't said anything more, given no other explanations.

Even if the Gods were lying, Pel was not telling them the truth either. Heldith had to do what was right here, not just what he wanted. He had come here with a mission and had no doubts in his head back then.

Why should he be so wracked with doubts now? It made no sense.

Should he run to Pel and confront him? Confront him with what? In his eagerness to know about Zeityl, he had forgotten that Ementiar and his siblings had condemned them to death if they failed. He was afraid to close his eyes, lest he fell into the vision again and give away his location to the Gods. It was obvious they couldn't see them here. Pelthiel's magic was powerful enough to stop even the Gods. He was aware of a proud smile curling his lips, though he had no idea why.

"Did you have another nightmare?" Sivreth asked, his voice so low as to be nearly inaudible. It still startled Heldith.

"You're awake?" he asked.

"I woke up just now. Did you have another nightmare?"

"A vision," he whispered back. "Ementiar."

He heard the gasp from Sivreth. "What did he say?"

"That they wouldn't rest till they had killed Pelthiel," he said. "That Pelthiel had killed their brother."

"Utfer?" Sivreth asked, "But he's still alive, isn't he?"

"No, not Utfer," Heldith couldn't explain why he was so reluctant to speak the name. "Zeityl."

"I've never heard the name," Sivreth said, sounding uncertain. "I know we don't know all the Gods, but I'm sure we've heard all the names at least once."

"He's dead. I told you," Heldith said. "The Gods claim Pelthiel did it."

"You don't believe them," Sivreth said.

Heldith thought of his recurring dream, of Pel pulling him out of the water, calling him by the name of a dead God, and he thought of the way Pel had talked about his death.

"No, I don't," he said. "I don't think I trust the Gods

anymore."

"I know how you feel," Sivreth said slowly. "But if they were able to contact you, maybe they could find you, find him. Shouldn't we warn him?"

"What are they going to do?" Heldith asked. "Send another poor sod here to fight him? It's not like they're going to fucking come down and face him."

He couldn't help his contempt from bleeding into the words. Sivreth chuckled.

"You've really turned around, haven't you? I always said Pelthiel wasn't the villain he was made out to be," Sivreth said, sounding almost smug.

"There's still Nagir," Heldith reminded him.

"Do you think he'll tell us if we ask him?" Sivreth asked, sounding hesitant.

"I don't know," Heldith said. "He has no reason to."

"You're right. But I want to know."

"We can ask," Heldith muttered. "Just... I hope he won't be angry."

He didn't know why that bothered him, except it did. He didn't want Pel to be angry at him, or upset, or disappointed.

"Why should he be?" Sivreth murmured. "He'll understand. Anyone would be curious."

True, but Pel didn't need to indulge their curiosity. They had come to kill him, and he had kept them alive. What right had any of them to ask anything of him? Even questions? Heldith said nothing as he listened to Sivreth's breathing evening out. He sighed and stared up at the ceiling. He couldn't see anything, but he could still hear the sounds of the rain outside. The sound of thunder was muffled now. Probably Pelthiel's wards had an added layer to them.

He could imagine the night sky, the dark clouds with the

streaks of lightning and the torrential downpour and Hamithia riding the storm, her dark hair flying behind like a banner and her dark clothes making her indistinguishable from the clouds, the band of gold around her head shining more brightly than anything.

What?

Where had that come from? Hamithia was a God, but why should she be riding the storm and why the fuck would he be imagining her? Heldith swallowed. What was happening to him? Was it another vision? He hoped not. Would the Gods be able to find him? He was certain they would not, but Sivreth's words had brought doubts, and he didn't want doubts. Heldith wanted to be certain. He was a fool to ever pray to Ementiar. He had not thought it held any danger to Pel.

*Don't lie!*

So, perhaps he wasn't completely unaware of the dangers. After all, he knew the Gods wanted Pel dead, but he had been so desperate for answers that he had been ready to ignore them.

*And what answer did I get that I didn't have before?*

He knew now why the Gods really wanted Pel's death. It wasn't about Nagir at all. Not even about Utfer. It was only about Zeityl and whatever part the Gods believed Pelthiel had played in his death. Revenge. That was what it was all about, ultimately. He and his friends were just pawns in this game. What about the ones before them? The ones who had been sacrificed to Utfer? All because of what? Did any of this even have a purpose anymore?

A sudden clap of thunder drummed in his ears, and the earth shook as if from its impact. Heldith was out of his bed the next instant, his warrior's instinct making him reach for his sword. Blood was drumming in his ears. He was certain that this was no ordinary thunderclap.

"What was that?" Kiriel asked, leaping up and grabbing

his sword, tension radiating off him in waves.

"I had a vision from Ementiar earlier," Heldith said. "I think the Gods found us, and I think they've decided to take a more direct role in this."

"About fucking time," Kiriel muttered.

"You're going to let them kill him?" Amerla demanded, up as well, her sword in her hand, and her eyes flashing.

"Don't be ridiculous," Kiriel said. "A few weeks ago, sure, but not now, not after knowing they were just playing with us."

"They dragged us into this feud," Sivreth said. "Let's show them we can do more than be their toys."

The door was flung open as they approached it, and they could see Pelt standing outside, the rain swirling around him. He was dry, not even his hair moving. Facing him stood two people Heldith had never seen in his life before, but he recognised them for all that.

"Abityl and Hamithia," he whispered. Hamithia looked the same as in the brief vision he had had. Abityl was dressed all in gold as if to contrast with his sister; even his skin was gold.

Heldith walked out into the storm, casting a spell to keep the rain off him, and reached Pel's side, and he wasn't the only one. The four of them stood, two to a side, their swords and magic at the ready.

"You turn against us?" Abityl spoke.

"You lied to us!" Sivreth said. "You used us. He was the only one to tell us the truth!"

"Kill him!" Hamithia said. "And we'll fulfil every one of your wishes!"

None of them moved.

"Kill him!" Hamithia screamed. "Or I'll kill every last person you love!"

"And you wonder why they turn against you." Pelthiel's

voice was quiet, but they all heard it.

"I mean it!" Hamithia said. "I will see every last one of your loved ones sacrificed to Utfer if you don't kill him *right now*." Her voice had gone quiet too and her eyes moved across them. "Your wife, Amerla. Belania, is it not? Your sister, Kiriel. Aderla. Your brother, Sivreth. Fedytiel, the one you had fought so hard to protect all your life. Your friend, Heldith. Ryrthin. They will all die if you do not obey us now."

The icy coldness of her voice made it clear that she meant it.

"They couldn't defeat me before," Pel said. "What makes you think they can now?"

Heldith noticed with dismay that his friends were moving away, forming the position they had when they had cast the truth spell. He looked at Pel, who looked back at him, seemingly unconcerned about the Gods.

"Do what you have to," he said.

"Heldith," Kiriel called, and Heldith saw the determination on his face, as well as something else. "They will kill our people," Kiriel said.

Heldith moved, taking his position in the last corner. Pelthiel stood in the centre, still and steady. The four of them looked at the granite hard faces of the Gods, and at each other. They cast the spell together, and it hit Pel at the same time, causing him to stumble and fall on to the ground, on his knees and hands.

Triumphant smiles bloomed on the Gods' faces.

# TWENTY FIVE

Pel was in a world of pain, and memories bloomed in his mind. He was vaguely aware of the spell, of his recollections it brought to the fore. He had been expecting an attack, but not this, this violation of his deepest and most sacred remembrances.

Leithia!

He tried to hold on to them, to keep her hidden, but the spell had him helpless. He couldn't help but be proud of the four youngsters, even as he was angry. They were quick-thinking and ingenious. Strong and intelligent. Perhaps it had been a mistake to spare them and to keep them, but he could not have hurt them anymore than he could have ripped out his own heart. Even now, given a chance, he wouldn't hurt them any more than he would need to, to subdue them.

Had he truly thought he had buried his heart? With Leithia, with Nagir and all his regrets, with Zeityl?

Zeityl!

A fresh wave of panic broke in him, but he was as helpless against the tide of memories as Zeityl had been against the ocean.

Pel fought, struggled till his world disappeared and the darkness took him. But the memories rolled over him still.

The memories of that day, of his parting from Zeityl, and Pel had returned to that island where he had saved Zeityl, where he had said goodbye to him. He has stayed there, not knowing the truth till a week later when he had woken up in the middle of the night, breath choking, and heart clenching so tight.

He had run to the beach to see Zeityl stand there.

"This is all I can do for you now," he had said, before he fell into the waves, and Pel had leapt in after him, but Zeityl was gone, and Serityl had refused to give him up.

Pel gasped as he came to. He was still on the beach. The rain was still coming down in torrents, the fury of the storm crashing against the barrier of magic that enveloped all of them. Dimly, he was aware that the youngsters had taken their place by his side again, that Heldith was kneeling by his side, and that there was a hand on his cheek, caressing his face.

"This is your doing," he whispered to Heldith.

"I'm sorry," Heldith said softly, his touch so light, but it left burning trails on Pel's skin. "I couldn't let them hurt you. I couldn't let them hurt anyone."

Heldith was already so strong, and it should have been worrying, but it was not. It was familiar and expected. Pel closed his eyes again, tired. He didn't think it was going to help, but at least it would content Heldith.

He was aware of a growl that broke from the throats of the two Gods.

"What is this?" Abityl asked, his voice as reverberating as the thunder which rolled overhead.

"His memories," Heldith said, facing them. "You said he killed Zeityl. That is why you want his death. I want you to see that he didn't!"

"You don't know that," Pel whispered, surprised and touched by the conviction in his voice.

"I know you," Heldith answered, stealing away Pel's breath. "I know you wouldn't have killed him, not when..."

"Not when what?" Pel asked.

"You loved him, didn't you?" Heldith asked, his voice quiet. "Zeityl."

Pel closed his eyes again, familiar grief threatening to spill over into the empty spaces inside him where his sister had once lived, where Zeityl had once been.

"Did I?" he asked.

"He loved you," Heldith sounded bewildered as he spoke. "I don't know how I know that, though."

Pel wanted to scream, to cry, but he didn't. "Why would you do this to me?" he whispered.

"There was no other way," Heldith said. "They would never stop, not as long as they thought you had killed him. He chose to die for you... They had to see that."

"Do you think they will care for the distinction?" Pel asked. He felt so weak, so tired. "On most days, even I blame myself."

Heldith's hand stilled, and dropped, making Pel miss its warmth. "Zeityl wouldn't have wanted that."

"You don't know that," Pel said, though he wasn't right. Heldith did know, and if he said that, it had to be true.

"I do," Heldith said, again sounding confused. "I am certain that Zeityl never wanted you to blame yourself. He made the choice because he knew..."

"Knew what?" Pel asked.

Heldith looked confused. "I don't know..." he said. "It's gone... I don't know what happened."

"It doesn't matter anyway," Pel muttered.

It really didn't. Whatever Zeityl might have wanted, whatever he might have thought, whatever he believed, the fact was Pel could never stop blaming himself even when he was angry at Zeityl.

The spell hit him the next moment.

# TWENTY SIX

Heldith saw the rage on the Gods' faces and the resignation on his friends'. They had cast a simple binding spell, and he had turned it into this, fuelled by Pel's own magic. Perhaps it was wrong of him, but he couldn't see a way out of it. The magic bound all seven of them. The Gods weren't going anywhere till this was over. Outside of the circle of magic, he was aware of the renewed fury of the storm, of vague shapes moving through the rain. The other Gods had come to join the fight, but the magic was keeping them out, Pel's magic, fed by each of theirs, and reinforced by the very elements. Heldith didn't know how he had cast a spell like that, from where it came, but he had no time to wonder about it as a fresh wave of Pel's memories washed over them.

The memory fragmented and fell apart as Pel's will surged to fight the intrusion.

"Don't," Heldith whispered, his heart aching and his hand still on Pel's face. "Don't fight it, please. The Gods need to see. They need to know. They'll never leave you alone till they do."

"End me," Pel whispered. "I don't fear them, and I don't

care for them. Just end me!"

"You know I can't," Heldith said, anguish at the expression on Pel's face overwhelming him. "I have to save you."

"It's too late for that," Pel whispered before he lost consciousness, and there was nothing but the rain and the darkness and the emptiness where the spell had been.

Pel had broken free of it, broken it with a surge of power that had drained him. Heldith was aware of his friends closing ranks before him, and of the rain pelting them. The Gods were all there, and all that stood between them and their quarry were the four of them.

"Now that that travesty is over," one of the Gods spoke. Heldith couldn't see who it was, but the slightly nasal voice brought forth a name from the recesses of his memory. Aristyl's voice continued, "Will you come to your senses and kill him, or must we put an end to everything you hold dear?"

Was this what it meant to be the chosen of the Gods? Where he had to make a choice between his family and Pel? Heldith didn't know what stopped him, but to choose to end Pel was unthinkable. He heard his friends shifting their positions.

*They won't choose him!*

Why would they, anyway? Pel might have spared their lives, even saved them, but he was still a stranger, and the love that they held in their hearts for their families was stronger than any bond of gratitude. They would have given their lives for Pel's, but none of them would sacrifice the lives of those they loved.

"Why don't you kill him yourself?" Sivreth asked, "He's right there, he's helpless. Why must his blood be on our hands?"

"Because they can't," Heldith said as he rose.

His friends turned to look at him. He looked down at Pel and something filled him, a deep anguish, a grief he could not name or explain.

"They cannot kill any of us. They need us to kill for them." He straightened and looked at the Gods. "That all ends today."

He moved forward till he was abreast with his friends. "You won't hurt us or our loved ones. You can't. You can send visions and dreams, but that is all the power you have when you're here, with his magic on one side and the ocean on the other."

He didn't know from where the words came; it was as if it was knowledge that was in his very bones and it was coming forth now. Even visions and dreams were going to take much of the Gods' strength while here.

"And," he added. "You are not leaving here without knowing the truth."

"You have no power over us!" Amythia spoke, her bronze armour shining brightly even in the darkness. Despite her words, there was worry on her face and all the other Gods looked anxious as well as shocked.

Fools! Thoughtless fools!

Heldith was aware of grief rising in him, grief for their grief, their impulse that had led them here without knowledge, but he was certain of one thing. None of the Gods could leave. None of their powers would avail them. They were as helpless as the unconscious man on the ground. He looked at his friends.

"They won't hurt anyone now," he said. He went back to where Pel lay and lifted him in his arms. "Let us go back to the house."

He knew that the Gods were following too, but he could not care about it now.

He laid Pel down on his bed after drying him and changing his clothes. He and his friends went to their room to dry themselves and change afterwards. None of them said anything about the Gods waiting in the large front room.

"Heldith," Kiriel said slowly. "How do you know all that?"

Good question. He wished he had an answer.

"I don't know how I know," he said, rubbing his forehead. His head was throbbing. "It was... I don't know, like remembering some things you had forgotten... you know, like you see or hear or smell something and suddenly you remember something that you had forgotten for so long? It was like that, but I don't know anything more."

They went to the front room where the Gods were. Heldith knew them all. Utfer with his pale blue eyes and sallow skin, Amythia with her bronze armour and swarthy complexion, Hamithia who rode the storms in her dark clothes with her skin and eyes and hair all blending perfectly amongst the rain clouds that she loved, Abityl with his golden skin and armour, Aristyl with his stooped form and beautiful face, Ementiar with his weathered face and short stature, Brolar with his deep grey eyes and white clothes, Poltiel whose appearance changed with his reckless nature and anger, Keithia with her wide eyes and cunning nature, Pitoryl with his milky skin and wisdom. They were all familiar to him, and yet he could not say how.

"How did you keep us here?" Pitoryl asked. "How can a mortal possess such power?"

"It's not me." Heldith rubbed his forehead again. The throbbing was a pounding now. "It's him."

"Pelthiel?" Ementiar asked. "Even he doesn't possess that power."

"Not him," Heldith said, feeling nauseous now besides the hammering in his head, which felt like it was going to break apart from the inside. "Zeityl."

"He's dead!" It was Utfer who spoke, his hoarse voice

throbbing with pain and anger. "Pelthiel killed him!"

"He isn't dead," Heldith said. "He cannot be. None of you can be killed. You're immortal. Even Serityl cannot kill you, though she may hold you fast in her embrace for good."

As soon as he spoke the words, he knew who Serityl was, and his headache worsened, leading him to clutch it.

"Heldith!" Amerla sounded concerned. "Heldith, what is wrong?"

Heldith sank to his knees, clutching his head, the pain blinding in its intensity. He was aware of nothing except his head. There was a scream, and it was coming from him. He saw himself lying inside a darkened room, and as the memory surfaced, he lost consciousness.

*Zeityl looked at the young siblings talking, just outside the house, in the garden. He couldn't hear what was being said, and he didn't want to. He could guess. A sneer twisted his face. It had been so easy to fool the young man! Just a made-up story and now, all Pelthiel wanted was to help him. He would probably rope in his sister in his quest. She was powerful, as powerful as their father had been, but he couldn't tell anything about Pelthiel's power. Perhaps he wasn't so powerful. But there was no doubt that Leithia was a threat, as much of a threat as their father had been. His journey had not been wasted.*

*His frowning glance fell on the mortals again. They had saved him from the ocean. That was a part of their plan that had been unexpected. He should have remembered that Serityl had a long memory and an even greater ability to hold grudges. It was strange how weak he still was. It was a lowering realisation that Serityl was more powerful than him, perhaps more powerful than all of them together. Her rage and vengeance had turned her into a force that they couldn't subdue. Perhaps they should have left her siblings alone. It was too late for regrets now. They had been young and drunk with their own power and they had thought themselves invincible.*

*He pushed the unwelcome thoughts away. Serityl had had her revenge, but she would not be satisfied till they were all gone. Well, she would not get her chance. They had all the time in the universe to grow more powerful and one day, they would be more powerful than her and on that day, they would once again be able to roam this world at will.*

*He heard footsteps approaching, and he closed his eyes, pretending to be asleep. At least he didn't have to pretend to be weary. Pain was a different matter altogether, though. It was something he didn't have experience with and that made pretence slightly difficult. But it was not impossible. After all, he was a God, and those he was attempting to fool were only mortals.*

*"He's asleep." Pelthiel's voice drifted to his ears.*

*"Let him sleep," Leithia spoke, sounding troubled. "I'll leave the medicine here."*

*"Leit, we have to help him."*

*"How Pel? Even we can't take on all of Nagir by ourselves. Or protect his people. We're not Gods, Pel. There are limits to what we can do."*

*"You said it yourself, Leit. What is the point in having all this power if we can't help anyone?"*

*"Pel, we are helping people. We saved him from a certain death. But there are limits to our power, to what we can do. I want to help him, I do, but-"*

*Zeityl decided to make his move. He moaned as if in pain and opened his eyes.*

*"I'm sorry," he said apologetically. "If you can use your magic to help me get to Nagir in time, that's all I want. Please."*

*Leithia came closer, and he could see the determination on her face. "Pel and I didn't risk our lives to save yours just so you can throw it away."*

"*My life already belongs to Utfer,*" he argued. "*What if he chooses to punish you for saving me?*"

"*I'm sure he would have preferred his sacrifice not to be drowned,*" Pelthiel said with a small smile. "*Don't worry. Gods have better things to do than to meddle in human affairs.*"

*Zeityl gave an inward roll of his eyes. How naïve these humans were!*

Heldith stared up at the ceiling. He was on a couch, still in the front room. His friends were with him. The Gods were also there, standing away from them.

"What was that?" Sivreth asked.

"What happened?" he asked.

"Your eyes glazed over, and you kept saying Pelthiel's name," Sivreth said. "What happened, Heldith?"

Heldith wished he knew.

145

# TWENTY SEVEN

P el woke suddenly and was reassured at finding
himself in his room. Was it all a dream then? Yet,
he could feel them. A look of distaste crossed his
face as he got up. He was weak. It had taken all his magic, all his
reserves, to break that damn spell. What had Heldith been trying
to do, anyway? He could feel his magic inside him. He wasn't as
recovered as he would have liked to be, but it would have to do.
The first thing to do would be to get rid of his unwelcome guests
and of the young fools, as well. Let the Gods sacrifice them to
Utfer! He didn't care!

*What about Heldith?*

What about him? Pel opened the door to his room and
stepped out, leaning against the wall for an instant. He was
apparently the only one to recognise who Heldith was. Heldith
might be beginning to remember, but once away from this island
and the source of his memories, he might not remember so
quickly. It was a mistake to let him stay, perhaps. After all, who
could have managed to end him? Pel had been greedy, and he had
paid the price. Heldith had violated his mind, his memories, and
no matter what his intentions, it was unforgivable.

*I should have known better.*

Would he never learn? Had all his memories, his experiences, taught him nothing? He should have kicked him out as soon as he realised who he was. But he had been weak; he had not wanted to send him back to face certain death.

Pel pushed himself away from the wall and started walking towards the front room.

*He would have come back and found another way to torment me!*

It was with his anger boiling inside that he walked into the front room. Heldith was on the couch with Amerla kneeling beside him, and Sivreth and Kiriel hovering by the couch anxiously. The Gods stood ranged against the far wall.

"What the fuck are you still doing here?" he growled at them, his fury at seeing them here causing whatever little control he had to slip.

They had been the architects of Leithia's death, of the destruction of his old life. Of everything he had lost. They were the ones who were ultimately responsible for what happened to Zeityl.

"We can't leave," one of them said.

Pel did not know who any of them were. He didn't know any of them by appearance, and he didn't want to.

"What do you mean, you can't leave?" he snarled. "You're Gods!"

"Something is preventing us," another said, his eyes flickering to Heldith an instant before moving back to Pel.

"Is this your doing?" Pel asked Heldith, turning to him, his fury not abating one jot.

"It is his," Heldith said. "Zeityl's. You know he's not dead, don't you?"

Pel nodded, shock draining out his fury. "How do you

know?"

"I don't know." Heldith sounded afraid and confused. "It's like, things just come to me and I don't know from where they came or how… it's not visions…it's *knowledge*."

The truth burned Pel's tongue, but he would not speak it, not with so many people around.

"Do you know why they can't leave?"

"He… he didn't die," Heldith said, speaking haltingly, as if unsure. "But he did sacrifice himself, and he did it so you would be safe from them… if they found you, if they approached you, they would be powerless to leave or to do you harm… he bound his sacrifice with his power, and his love, and only he can break it."

Pel took a deep breath, his mind trying to wrap itself around what he heard, his thoughts chaotic, trying to make sense of what he heard.

"Are you saying they can't leave here *ever*?"

Heldith's eyes met his. "Yes. Not unless you let them go."

"A moment ago, you said only he can break whatever protective spell he cast."

"The spell, yes, but you can choose to let them go. But if they return, they'll still be powerless and they'll be trapped."

"If I let them go," Pel said slowly, "if I let them out into the world again, they'll just keep on doing what they've been doing so far. Sending innocent kids after me and killing them if they fail."

Heldith said nothing.

"What happens if I leave?" Pel asked.

"They'll be free," Heldith said.

It was just like Zeityl. Even his attempts to protect him were screwing him over.

"If they go free, the first thing they are likely to do is

make good on their promise to destroy everything and everyone you love," Pel said.

Heldith swallowed, comprehension and horror dawning on his face. The Gods were tense too, though Pel could see the resignation on their faces. They had no reason to expect mercy, not from him, not after everything they did.

"You can't!" Heldith said, the words bursting from him.

"I don't have a choice," Pel said. "Besides, it would mean you all can finally go home. Isn't it what you want?"

"You're talking of staying here and holding them here," Amerla said. "Forever."

"For as long as I live, certainly," Pel agreed.

"Heldith is right," Kiriel said. "You can't. You can't just... there has to be another way."

"I'm not strong enough to bind them here," Pel said. "And I would rather not have any more deaths on my conscience. This is the best option for all."

"We'll bind ourselves," one of the Gods spoke. "Don't keep us here! We will bind ourselves not to hurt these humans or their loved ones. We will not send anyone after you ever again."

"I wish I could trust you," Pel said quietly. "Unfortunately, I don't. I trusted your brother once, and he betrayed me. I'm not about to make the same mistake again." He turned to the four champions. "And as for you, you are all free to leave. I would really appreciate it if you are gone before sundown tomorrow."

"You don't have to do this for us," Sivreth said.

"Look," Pel said. "I live alone on a deserted island. This is not a sacrifice for me. So, stop speaking nonsense, all right?"

"This is revenge, isn't it?" one of the Gods spoke, their voice bitter. "You... we took your sister, and you took our brother... can't you let it go at that?"

"Like you did all these years?" Pel asked, his fury building again. "Besides, I didn't take your brother. Whatever Zeityl did was by his choice. And Leithia wasn't the only family you took from me."

He turned to Heldith. "I've a charm that should keep you safe from the ocean. Don't forget to take it before you leave."

Heldith was looking at him with an expression of hurt betrayal. His face was pale and his eyes wide. Pel turned away from the gaze, feeling inexplicably guilty.

*Why should I feel guilty? He is the one who screwed me over!*

Pel walked away, not sparing a backward glance at Heldith. He needed rest, to replenish his magic. Heldith was already behind him, part of a past he had no desire to cling to.

# TWENTY EIGHT

The storm died out sometime near noon, but Heldith didn't notice. Sivreth was the only other person who was not enthusiastic about leaving, but it had more to do with the fact that his parents were abusive rather than anything else. Heldith didn't have any excuse for not wanting to go back. It wasn't that he didn't want to see his parents or Ryr again, but he didn't want to leave Pel. He knew he would never be able to find this island again once he left. Pelthiel's magic would ensure that.

He had nothing to pack except the clothes he wore and the weapons he had brought. The only thing Pelthiel had taken was the compass given by the Gods, the magical compass that the Gods had given him. Without it, he could never come back.

*Why do I even want to come back?*

That was something for which he couldn't find an answer. He didn't know what these feelings were that he had towards Pel, feelings that were never encouraged and certainly not reciprocated. He still remembered the fury on Pel's face the night before. Or had it been early this morning? It made no difference.

Heldith knew that part of that fury had been directed at him, though Pel had said no word. Heldith could see it, the condemnation in Pel's eyes that he had not uttered. He had thought he was trying to save Pel by casting that spell, but Pel hadn't needed his protection. He already *had* protection.

Jealousy surged in him. What call did he have to be jealous of Zeityl? The God might not be dead, but he was no more. Whatever it was he did, it was irreversible. Irrevocable. He had ensured Pel's safety from his siblings far better than any paltry spell of Heldith's could.

*If only I had known!*

But he hadn't; that knowledge had come to him too late. After he had cast the spell, exposed Pel's buried memories and held them up for everyone to see.

"End me," Pel had begged him.

End him rather than violate his mind, and yet he hadn't listened.

Perhaps it was good that he was leaving.

He looked outside where Pel was standing by the ocean. Was he talking to Serityl? Or to Leithia? Or Zeityl? He swallowed as he looked at the room. This had been his home, and he had been content here for a while. Perhaps Pel was not talking to Zeityl. Hadn't he said Zeityl had betrayed him? And he had seen that memory, though it was not Pel's memory. Why had it come to him?

*"Betrayal comes naturally to you, doesn't it?"*

Pel's words rang in his ears and the sword that he was trying to buckle on fell from his suddenly nerveless fingers. He stared at it as it fell but an inch from his foot. Would it have wounded him?

He rose. He had to know, and there was only one person he could ask. But this time, if Pel refused him answers, he was not going to push, or try to find them another way. It was that which had landed him in this situation in the first place.

"You look like you've seen a ghost," Sivreth said.

"I need to talk to Pelthiel," he said.

"Heldith," Kiriel said. "I've not said anything till now, but... please. This isn't real, you know. What you feel for him. You've been trapped here, and he was kind to us, and that's all this is."

"Kiriel," Heldith sighed. "I wish I can reassure you, but I don't know what my feelings for him are, so how can I say anything? I need to talk to him, all right?"

He ran out of the house, ignoring the Gods who were still huddled together in the front room, though his heart went out to them too. Their misery was palpable, cloaking them like a blanket, and he hated how much it hurt him.

*They deserve it!*

He wished he could convince himself of it.

"Pelthiel," he called even before he reached the man.

Pel turned to face him, and Heldith was shocked at how haggard he looked. It was as if he had aged ten years in a few hours.

"What is it, Heldith? Is it the charm? It's in the house,"

"It's not about the charm," he said, his heart beating fast. "I needed to ask you something."

Pel lifted an inquiring brow.

"You said that day when we cast that truth spell, that betrayal came naturally to me. What did you mean by that?"

Pel's eyes slid away from his. "I must have been angry," he said.

"Zeityl betrayed you," Heldith said. "And I suddenly know things about him that no one else does... I remember his memories... and you... you accused me of betraying you as if I'd done it before..."

Pel remained silent, though now his eyes were meeting his
Heldith couldn't read his expression.

"Am I Zeityl?" Heldith asked, desperate.

Again, Pel remained silent.

"Pelthiel-"

"It doesn't matter who you are," Pel said quietly. "You
betrayed me too, last night, when you forcibly revealed my
memories. I know you thought you were doing the right thing,
but I'm not a child, Heldith. I can take care of myself, like I have,
all these years. You violated my mind. That's as bad as anything
Zeityl had ever done."

"Am I him?" Heldith asked again, desperate, wanting
answers, and yet afraid.

"Now you are," Pel said. "Which is why you need to leave
Heldith. This... we... it was doomed from the beginning."

"How am I him?" Heldith couldn't recognise his own
voice.

"I don't know," Pel said. "It doesn't matter, anyway."

Heldith stared at him, unable to say anything. It seemed as
if he was in a nightmare. That he should have so spectacularly
messed things up was something he could not accept. Was he
beyond forgiveness? Beyond redemption? The expression on Pel's
face told him all he needed to know. Heldith had destroyed any
chance there was of their being together before it had ever begun.
Zeityl's sacrifice was for nothing in the end.

Zeityl didn't sacrifice himself for a second chance. He did
it to keep Pel safe.

Pel was safe, but was now stuck with a group of people he
hated with no way of escaping.

"Pelthiel," he said finally, not knowing what else to say.
There was a pain in his heart and there didn't seem to be enough

air in the world to fill his lungs.

Pel took a step forward, took his face between his hands, and kissed him on the forehead. "Goodbye, Heldith," he said.

# TWENTY NINE

P el thought he would spontaneously combust in fury. The Gods were still in his house. The entire island was free to them, and they had chosen to stay in his house.

*What did I ever do to deserve this?*

The bone deep loathing he had for them was a living thing inside him. It danced in his veins, sighed in his breath, and strengthened his resolve to kick them out.

Utfer's glance at him was full of speculation, and an equal measure of hatred, but there was also doubt there, as if he had encountered something he had never expected to. That expression nearly caused Pel's resolve to crumble, but he pulled himself together. He could not falter. Not against them.

*They killed Leithia.*

"You need to leave," he said. "I don't want you in my house."

"Where do we go?" Hamithia asked, her lost expression at odds with the belligerent tone of her voice.

"I don't fucking care," Pel snarled. "The whole island is there. Just stay away from me."

"You don't tell us what to do!" Abityl snapped.

"When you're in my house, I do," Pel said, glaring at them.

"Brother," Ementiar said as Abityl opened his mouth again. "He's right."

Pel crossed his arms across his chest. He was not going to be fooled by the Gods again, no matter how benign they might pretend to be. He had learned his lesson.

*Zeityl died for you.*

*If he loved me, he would have come back to me instead!*

*He did as Heldith, and you sent him away.*

His own mind taking sides and arguing was not a new thing, but there were times Pel couldn't ignore that. He had no answer to that last either. What was he supposed to do, anyway? Heldith was barely an adult. How could he have taken advantage of him?

*Zeityl is a God, not bound by age.*

Heldith was human, and he was not Zeityl, at least not completely.

The Gods trudged out, slumped shoulders and confused glances. Somehow, watching them leave didn't give him as much satisfaction as he had expected. There was relief, but not happiness.

*What did I expect?*

Berating himself was not going to get anything done, though. Pel stepped out of the house, staring at it dispassionately. He remembered building it, using his hands, without magic. He had used magic to shape the wood and stone, but brick by brick, he had built it himself. After all, he was alone, and he had time.

And then the first chosen one had come.

Avithian.

Eighteen years old, and full of righteous conviction. Pel

157

had been angry, but also amused. He had defeated him, taken his compass and had sent him on his way. Three years later, the next one had come. Silnia. The cycle had repeated every three years, till after he had sent Dystilan home. It was nearly three years later that Serityl had told him about a child who was at home in the ocean, a child who had a soul older than the world.

Pel was beginning to wish he had never made that trip, had never seen Heldith, had never learned of the fate of all the children he had defeated and sent on their ways. Two months after his return, Amerla had come and this time, he had kept her on the island, hoping that her not returning would stop the Gods. Of course, he should have known they wouldn't give up that easily.

All that was at an end now, but the house no longer was what it had been to him once. It was no longer his refuge, his sanctuary. Hands that were not his had touched it; it had memories of other people who weren't him.

Memories of someone he was better off forgetting. Would he never learn his lesson?

It had housed his worst enemies for two days.

Pel made a gesture, and the house crumbled where it stood, wood and brick and stone disintegrating into dust; not just the house, but everything within, everything except the books and scrolls that had been his only companions during the years he had spent alone.

"Why did you do that?" a soft voice spoke.

One of the Gods.

"None of your fucking business!" Pel said, turning to face the God.

"I'm only seeking to understand," Pitoryl said. "If... if what that boy said was correct, and it does look like it was, it means that our brother chose you over us, over himself, over everything... it means that our misguided attempts at revenge were... inappropriate."

Pel snorted. "That's what you call it? You killed those kids because they failed to do something that anyone would have known they wouldn't be able to! At least anyone with half a brain should have been able to know that."

"We misjudged the extent of your powers," Pitoryl said. "But I cannot apologise for the deaths of the champions. Their lives kept Utfer alive."

"And of course, his life is more important than those of four humans!"

Pitoryl tilted his head to a side, his eyes searching.

"Four mortal lives against an immortal one seemed like a straightforward choice."

"If he's immortal, he wouldn't die, anyway," Pel said, gritting his teeth against his rage.

"He can fade till there's nothing left of him, just a presence without substance," Pitoryl said. "We didn't think the lives of four mortals a heavy price to pay."

"And what about their families? The people who love them? How do you think they feel? Oh, that's right. It doesn't matter to you, does it? After all, they're all mortals too."

"And so are you," Pitoryl said. "Which means we won't be trapped here forever."

"You're so stupid," Pel said. Damn it, he was tired. So fucking tired of the Gods and their drama. "He sacrificed himself to keep you trapped here with me, bound your powers to mine. Have you considered that I could sacrifice myself to keep you trapped here forever?"

Pitoryl's chalky white face went even paler. "Are you going to?"

"If I have to," Pel said. "If he cannot come up with a

159

better solution."

"He is gone," Pitoryl said.

Pel shrugged. If they didn't recognise Heldith, he wasn't going to tell them. He had no expectation that Heldith would ever come back, not after how they had parted, but he could hope that he would at least find a way to get rid of his unwanted guests.

Pitoryl looked at where the house had stood. "Where will you live?"

"Not your concern," Pel replied with a finality that brooked no argument.

# THIRTY

The Gods were standing out in the open, looking more lost than he had ever seen them. Heldith felt his heart wrench at the sight despite the hostile glances that were directed at him. None of them even entertained the possibility that Zeityl and he could be connected, that they could be one... yet how was that even possible? If he was Zeityl, then Zeityl didn't really sacrifice himself, did he? How was it his protection spell still worked, then?

It scared him, the thought that Zeityl might still be trapped somewhere and his tortured mind and memories had somehow found him. Not that it mattered now, but it still meant that everything he had felt till then, everything he was feeling now, was Zeityl, not him. But even that would be better than him and Zeityl being one, because that meant there wasn't even a him. If he and Zeityl were one, it meant that all he was, was a repository of Zeityl's feelings, memories and experiences, that Heldith didn't really exist.

*I'm not even real and it still feels like my whole being is being ripped apart.*

He was being pathetic. What had he lost, in fact? He was going back home, safe and sound, and with no Gods in the world to fuck them over again. Heldith had made some new friends. He would see his home, his parents, and his best friend again soon.

"What happens to the world when you're stuck here?" he asked the Gods.

"They go on as ever," Ementiar said. "We aren't as necessary to the world as we'd had you believe. Sure, we can cause significant changes, but we haven't much, have we? You'll be at the mercy of the elements and the cosmic forces older than us, though."

"Whim of one powerful entity instead of another," Heldith mused. "I thought you destroyed everyone except Serityl."

"How do you know Serityl?" Amythia asked. "And how do you know any of the things that you know?"

Heldith swallowed, but shrugged. "I don't know how. I just do." He paused. "For what it's worth, I'm sorry."

Utfer's face darkened. "Pity from a human. That's all we need!"

"Pride has always been a fault with you, my brother," Pitoryl said quietly, though his eyes were fixed on Heldith's face, a questioning expression in them. "That is what led us here in the first place."

Heldith would have loved to stay and listen to the Gods' arguing, but he wasn't up to it. He made his way back to where his friends were still waiting, all of them dressed and ready. Heldith picked up his weapons and belted on his sword sheath, and shouldered his shield. He was leaving behind his bow and arrows. Even with magic, the journey could be long, and he didn't think the bow would survive it. The one he had brought here hadn't, and he had made this one while here. It seemed fitting to leave it here.

"Do you think we could ever find our way back here?" Sivreth asked as he looked around with a longing look.

"I don't think so," Amerla said. "His magic... it's powerful... we would never have found this place without the magical compass the Gods gave us."

"Don't forget this," Kiriel handed something to Heldith. The charm Pel had made for him, the one that would protect him from Serityl.

*What happens if I leave it behind?*

He took it and placed it inside his tunic pocket. "Thank you."

"It feels strange to be leaving," Amerla murmured, looking around, a wistful expression on her face. "It's been my home for so many years... I don't know what to expect back home..."

"They wouldn't have threatened her life if she'd moved on," Heldith said. "I'm sure she'll be waiting."

Amerla looked away as her eyes welled.

"Let's go," Kiriel said, his eyes too shining, but they held apprehension as well.

Heldith was the last to leave, behind Sivreth, who looked like he would have liked to stay. Heldith wished he could say something, but what was there to speak? He did not know the kind of household Sivreth grew up in. His own had been loving. Too loving perhaps, but Sivreth had scars on his body that had nothing to do with his career as a warrior. It was something Heldith had never been able to wrap his head around. But Sivreth was no longer a child; he was an adult, a chosen of the Gods. Surely, things would be different now?

The Gods were still where they stood, looking at them with barely concealed hostility and envy and also—was that

163

STOLEN FROM A DREAM

longing?

Heldith could understand it. They were stuck here; they, the all-powerful beings, were helpless while the mortals they had tried to use were free. He wished he could muster up more anger, even hatred, but all he could feel was a heart wrenching loss.

"He won't live forever," Abityl spoke as Kiriel reached the beach. "Pelthiel. We'll be free once he dies, and we'll be coming after you first."

That broke the dam of Heldith's anger, his grief and loss adding an intensity to his feelings that had never been there before.

"You never learn, do you?" he demanded. "Your own brother, the one who you claim to love, gave his life to keep Pel safe from you! Hasn't even that taught you anything? You killed his father and his sister and yet, all he did was to hide himself away instead of fighting you and yet, you couldn't leave him alone! When will you ever learn?"

"How do you know all this?" Hamithia's eyes were blazing with fury. "How dare you judge us!"

Suddenly Heldith didn't want to be here any longer, didn't want to be here when they inevitably realised the truth, didn't want to listen to anything, recriminations or expressions of love. He wasn't sure which one he feared more. All he knew was that it would happen eventually, and he just needed to leave when they didn't yet recognise him, when his love for them wasn't crippling him, when his feelings for Pel wasn't so overwhelming.

He pushed past his friends, almost running to get out of the island. Something was suffocating him, and he drew in lungfuls of the salt laden air and was promptly sick. He vomited till there was nothing left and yet he couldn't stop. He retched on an empty stomach, his insides feeling like they would like to leave

nis body as well. A hand was rubbing his back, and a voice was saying
,omething, but it was a while before he could recognise it.
"It'll be all right," Sivreth was saying. "Just let it all out."
Heldith was aware that his body was being wracked with
,obs as well. When had that happened? Amerla was kneeling by
nim, her hand on his shoulder. He straightened, wiping his mouth
nnd accepting the waterskin that Kiriel was holding out to him.
He drank as if he had been dying of thirst and gave his friends a
weak smile.

"Let us go home," he said.

# INTERLUDE II

P el watched the boat depart and felt nothing. This wasn't like the last time. The last time, he was the one leaving, and Zeityl was the one left behind. But then, both times, he was the one who ended up betrayed, so he didn't know why he didn't even feel hurt anymore. The cliff on which he stood was the highest point on the island, and he knew that if anyone in the boat looked back, they would be able to see him.

Why would they, though? Pel was grateful that they hadn't tried to kill him when they had the advantage, but that didn't justify the invasion of privacy he had suffered. Besides, as long as Zeityl's protection endured, there was no way that they could actually have harmed him. Not in any lasting way. Any killing or maiming spell they cast would have rebounded on them.

Pel was glad they hadn't tried anything like that. He might owe them nothing, but he had saved their lives, and would have been sorry to see them die. As it was, they had only wanted the Gods to know the truth. Rather, Heldith had wanted the

Gods to see that Pel hadn't killed Zeityl, that Zeityl had sacrificed himself to keep Pel safe.

How foolish of him to think that the truth would make any difference. The Gods didn't want the truth. They wanted their brother back, and failing it, they wanted someone to blame for it.

Just as Pel had blamed them for Leithia's death, had blamed the entirety of Nagir for that, and his anger and grief had caused the destruction of that city and its people. The knowledge of the havoc that he had wreaked had horrified him back then. It still did, a stone around his neck. He had hidden himself away here, because he didn't want to go back to the world, be with other people. He didn't want to do any more damage.

Back then, Pel had wanted revenge, but that was his fury, and his grief. The grief was still there, but time had dulled his anger, had given him perspective.

It was a pity that the Gods couldn't gain what he, a mortal, had gained.

Still, Pel knew that if they pushed him, he would destroy them. He wasn't that charitable or forgiving. Even for Zeityl's sake, he would not spare them.

*Give them to me*, Serityl said.

Pel chuckled. *Would you be able to hold them?*

*I don't think so*, she said, regretfully. *I can destroy them, but not hold them. I'm able to hold Zeityl because he isn't fighting me, and I am not destroying him for your sake.*

*I'm sorry*, Pel said. *I know that you want revenge, and because of me, you can't even have it.*

*It's not your fault, little one. I made the choice to spare Zeityl's soul and his life. His soul may be shattered and his life gone, but he still exists. His love for you is as much a reason why I chose to spare him as your love for him.*

*I can't force them out of here,* Pel said. *I may want to, but I can't.*

*You mean you won't.*

*I mean I won't,* Pel agreed. *I am not them, and I don't want to be. I hate them, but I don't want to kill them. Too many deaths have already happened.*

"Pelthiel," a voice spoke, and Pel turned around to see Abityl.

"What do you want?" Pel asked.

Abityl looked at him with an expressionless face. "What are you going to do with us?"

"Nothing," he said. "You stick to your side of the island, and I'll stick to mine. That way, neither of us should be tempted to destroy the other. Unless you want a battle."

"You think you can take us?" he sounded disbelieving.

"I know I can," Pel replied. "I can defeat you and even destroy you, but I don't want to. I hope you won't force my hand."

"You may not have killed our brother," Abityl said. "But you broke his heart, and that is the reason why he's dead. You may say it's not your fault, but it's your responsibility."

"You killed my sister!" Pel snapped. "As in, actually killed her. If anyone has a grievance here, it should be me."

*And Zeityl betrayed me and broke my heart,* he didn't say.

"What, all the people in Nagir not enough to pay for her life?" Abityl asked, his own anger seeming to rise. "Thousands of lives against your sister's and you still had to take our brother's as well?"

"I regret what I did to them," he said, not wanting to justify his own actions. "They didn't deserve it, but don't use my actions as a justification for your own. You have been sending *children* after me and killing them for failing. You never seem to understand anything other than your own wishes."

"You're no better than us!" Abityl snarled, taking a step forward, fists clenched. "How dare you preach to us!"

"I am no better," Pel agreed quietly. "But at least I know what I am, and I am capable of remorse and change. That's far more than all of you put together. Leave, Abityl. I have no wish to converse with you anymore."

Pel didn't wait to see if the God was gone, vanishing from the spot and going to the beach. Here, the Gods would not dare step foot. Here, they would not disturb him.

If he missed the four people who had been his companions for so long, he didn't want to think of it too much just yet.

# THIRTY ONE

Aderla wiped the sweat from her brow. It was not that she hated the work at the inn, but it was dreary. On occasion, a traveller might come with strange tales and songs, but such cases were rare. Their town was small, and though it was close to the Southern Isles, it was not near any of the major cities to be of interest to anyone, and it was not on the way to any of the major places, either.

The most excitement their town had had was when Kiriel was chosen by the Gods for a secret mission.

Aderla closed her eyes and breathed out. It always hurt to think of Kiriel. She didn't have much hope that he was still alive, after all these years, but her mother still held out hope. Her father had done the same, and had died for that hope, and nothing Aderla could say would change his mind.

She opened her eyes, blinked them furiously against the prickle of tears, and wiped the counter with unnecessary force.

"Are you okay?" a familiar voice asked, and she raised her eyes to look at Jinien. He was one of her coworkers at the inn, and someone she had known all her life.

"I don't know," she said. Jinien was one of the few people with whom she could be completely honest. "I want to say yes, but I don't know. I don't even know why... I just thought of Father, and I... I don't know what to do, Jinien... I want to leave, go somewhere, but Mother won't go, and I can't leave her."

Jinien nodded as if in understanding. Perhaps he did. If he did, it was more than she did. Her emotions were as much a jumble as her thoughts on most days. All she wanted was her father back and her brother back, but neither was possible.

"Sometimes I can't remember what he looked like," she said, her voice low. "Kiriel... I remember he used to smell of spices back then... spices, and sweat. I used to call it gross when he used to lift me in his arms. He was so big... so strong... he fought the kids that tried to bully me, he always got me whatever I wanted, climbed the tallest trees to get me fruits, and I... I can't remember his voice or his face now!"

"It has been years, Aderla," Jinien said softly. "You were a child back then... you can't be expected to remember everything."

"But he's my brother... how can I forget what he looked like? What he sounded like?"

"You remember how you made him feel," Jinien said. "Sometimes it's all we can do. On most days, I can't remember my ma either... but it's okay, you know? I remember how I felt when she was there, and it feels like she's still here with me."

"I want him back," Aderla whispered. "Not just in my mind, in my memories... I want him back, Jinien!"

She knew she sounded almost hysterical, and Jinien placed his hands on her shoulders.

"I know, Aderla," he said. "I'm sorry. I wish I could bring your brother and father back. I'm so sorry, Aderla."

She swallowed a sob and blinked back her tears again.

"You're helping more than you know."

If she didn't even have him to talk to, she was sure she would have gone mad. Her mother had enough worries of her own, and Aderla had few other friends.

"I'm glad," he said, before releasing her shoulders. "I should go open the inn now. Barlon will have our heads otherwise."

She laughed, feeling her insides warm and something within her growing lighter.

# Thirty Two

Kiriel could feel the dryness of his mouth as he approached his house. He had been dropped off in the port of the Southern Isles the previous day, and he had walked the rest of the way. It was already nearing night, and not many people were on the streets. No one even gave him a glance.

His heart was hammering in his chest as he knocked at his door. Trepidation filled him. It had been so many years since he had been gone. Would they even recognise him? Did his parents still live in this house? Aderla must be grown now, and at that thought, pain lanced through him. He had missed his sister's entire childhood.

The door was opened by a young woman who stared at him in enquiry.

"Yes?" she asked.

If he stared hard, he could see something of the little girl he had left behind.

"Aderla?" His voice came out in a croak.

She stared at him before her eyes widened and her hand

flew to her mouth.

"Kiriel!" Her voice was high, and she stared at him with wide eyes. "You're back!"

He nodded, unsure of what to do. He wanted to hug her, but would she even allow it? Was she someone who liked hugs?

"Kiriel?" The soft voice was familiar, though it had been years since he had heard it. He felt his vision blur as he looked at his mother.

"Mother..."

His voice was a whisper as he took a step forward. Aderla had moved out of the way and his mother was in front of him, her hands trembling as they reached up to touch his face.

"My son, my boy," she said, her voice choking with emotion as she cupped his face, her eyes on his face, tears flowing down her face. "My darling boy!" Her hands were moving on his arms, his chest, his hair, his face as if she was making sure he was indeed here. "Oh, my boy!"

He hugged her, unable to help it, crushing her to his chest, his own tears flowing freely. He couldn't remember himself crying like this ever.

"Mother," he said again. "Mother."

He just wanted to keep on saying it. When he was on that island, he had been certain he would never get to see her, or call her ever again.

*Pelthiel sacrificed himself so I can have this.*

His mind shied away from the thought. His erstwhile captor might claim it was no sacrifice, but the fact was, he was trapped on an island with a group of powerful beings who wanted nothing more than to kill him. They might be powerless for the moment, whereas his magic was still intact, but they could still push him off a cliff or stick a sword into him or drown him or do any number of things to him.

*I can't do anything about it. I have to think about my life now.*

"I'm back," he said, his arms holding his mother closer.

Kiriel didn't want to think of Pelthiel or the Gods or anything. He was home. He had his life back. This was his reality.

His mother released him.

"You're so grown," she said. "My son, my boy. Have you had dinner?"

She was wiping her eyes, and the question threw him off balance. He hadn't eaten anything for hours.

"No." He shook his head. He was hungry, but he did not want to eat.

"I'll set the table," Aderla said; she was still staring at him with wide eyes. Did she even remember him?

His mother made him sit at the table, and Aderla brought a pot of stew and some bread. Kiriel took a bite and choked as memories rushed into him, memories associated with this flavour this taste, this fragrance. It tasted like his childhood and adolescence, and all the happy days he had spent here before the Gods had chosen him and sent him off to fight a battle not his own.

Bitterness flooded his mouth, which he swallowed.

"Where's Father?" he asked. Was he in bed already? Why hadn't Mother called him?

"Oh, Kiriel," his mother whispered, her lips trembling. "I'm so sorry, my dearest. He departed this world two years ago."

Kiriel stared at her, his mind unable to comprehend what she had just said. His father gone? He was stuck on that island, and...

*The fucking Gods could have warned me!*

There was no way they wouldn't have known, and they hadn't told him. Of course they hadn't. Why should they? It didn't matter to them, not any more than he did. People died all he time, after all.

"How?" he asked.

"The wasting sickness." It was Aderla who answered. "He caught it from one of the people he treated, and... it was quick..."

"He could have moved into the mountains," Kiriel said, bewildered. That was what his father had always advised those with the sickness to do. "Why didn't he?"

"He didn't want to," his mother said, her gaze on the chair on which he used to sit. "Don't worry about it."

Kiriel frowned, his appetite gone. What did his mother mean? Why were both she and Aderla not meeting his eyes? What were they keeping from him? Kiriel was sick of secrets. The Gods had kept secrets and so had Pelthiel. And now, even his mother and his sister were-

*Oh*

It struck him then, what they were not telling him, why they avoided his eyes, why his father had refused to go to the mountains.

Nausea churned in his gut and he rose, pushing his chair back.

"I'm not hungry," he said. "I... can I sleep?"

"Take my room," Aderla said. "I'll clean your room and get it ready in the morning. I will sleep with mother tonight."

He wanted to say he would clean his room, but he found words had deserted him. He nodded, his throat closed and his chest tight, his whole being crying out, a cry that was echoing in the hollow spaces of his heart where his father had been. It was as if someone had his heart in a vice like grip and was trying to tear it from his chest. He felt and yet did not.

*Is this even real?*

# THIRTY THREE

B elania placed a hand over her belly and smiled softly. Her child was growing in there, and she could feel her move.

"Amerla," she murmured. "Are you well in there?"

It was bittersweet, naming her child after the woman she had once been married to. It still hurt somewhere deep in the recesses of Belania's heart that she had lost Amerla, but there was nothing she could do. The Gods had chosen her, and she was lost to Belania now.

Back then, Belania didn't think she would ever find love again, but she had. Drelin who had known her all her life, and loved her for most of it. He had loved Amerla too, she knew. The two of them had laughed about it once, the fact that Drelin loved them both. They had cared for him as a friend, but they never had eyes for anyone else.

But she had Drelin now, and Belania was happy. They both missed Amerla, and neither of them had thought twice when the augur told them that their child was a girl before deciding to name her Amerla.

"Belania," Drelin's voice shook her out of her reverie, but

before she could rise, he was inside the room, his smile wide and joyful. "I got a place in the harbourmaster's office," he said. "It's not as hard work as in the shop, and the pay is better. I would have more time to spend with you and Amerla now."

She laughed softly and placed a hand on his cheek. "I love you," she said. "But why do I get the feeling that you would still have taken this job even if the pay had been less?"

"It would still have been worth it to spend time with you and our daughter," he said. "As it is, I will be able to give you both everything you deserve and more."

She smiled at him. "You're all I want," she said. "You and our child. Nothing more."

But it was a lie, wasn't it? There was Amerla, the one she had loved first, the one she could never forget.

As if he understood her unspoken words, he drew her in his arms and held her. "I know," he said. "I want the same, Belania. If she were to come back... if it was possible... do you think she would accept me as a part of your life?"

She frowned. "What are you talking about?"

"If she ever returns," he said. "If you want to go to her, you know I won't stop you. I want you to be happy, you and her, and our child. All I could want will be to have a place in your life, even if it's only as the father of your child."

"Silly man," she whispered, her heart aching. "I can never be happy without you now. Don't you know that?"

He kissed her.

"Will you be completely happy without her, though?" he asked, later, his fingers drawing lazy patterns on her full belly.

"If she comes back, perhaps not," Belania conceded. "But... let's be real, Drelin... it has been such a long time. Is it likely that she would ever be back?"

"She was chosen by the Gods," he argued. "Doesn't that

mean that she would have been successful in whatever she set out to do?"

"If she was, she would have been back. We don't know what they asked of her... we don't know anything..."

Belania had hated the Gods since Amerla left, though she had never spoken it aloud. But here, in the circle of Drelin's arms, her body still tingling from their lovemaking, the words slipped out without reservation.

"I hate them, Drelin... I hate them so much for taking her from me... What was so important that they couldn't do themselves but had to ask a human to do?"

Drelin held her. "I know," he said. "I wonder the same, but it's better for us not to ask too many questions. If the priests learn of it, we'll be in danger."

She nodded, subsiding. He was right, but that didn't mean she was happy about it. The Gods were tyrants, and their lives were at Their whim. No matter how much she might hate it, they had no choice right now.

A part of her wondered if she would have felt so strongly if they had not been responsible for her losing Amerla. But did it matter? Her eyes had been opened to the cruelty of the Gods, and she didn't think she could go back to feeling the same way about Them.

"I just miss her so much, Drelin," she said. Her husband was the most understanding man in the world because he only held her closer and kissed her on top of her head.

"I know, love. I do, too."

But there was nothing they could do. Amerla was gone, and no matter how much they missed her and mourned her, she was not going to be back.

Belania still had this, a husband who loved her and a child growing inside her. She just wished that they were enough to fill the empty space that Amerla had left behind.

# THIRTY FOUR

The port was busy and Amerla's heart was in her mouth as Heldith helped her ashore. They had dropped Kiriel off the previous day. Whatever enchantment Pelthiel had placed on the boat had brought them home without any mishaps. The sea had lain docile, and the skies had been clear and they had not even met a whale or a pirate vessel, only fair winds and the clear blue of the sky and the glassy water.

"You'll be fine," Heldith whispered to her. "They wouldn't have threatened her if something had happened to her."

Amerla wished she could believe it, but even if Belania was fine, it didn't mean she wouldn't have moved on; it had been nearly eleven years, after all. Even if she hadn't moved on, it was not as if they could just pick up where they had left off. Were they even the same people that they had been? She was not, so wasn't it reasonable to expect Belania might have changed too? They had married young, but they had thought they had time to grow together, and to learn and understand each other's changes.

*Now, we're strangers who are married to each other.*

182

The thought was disturbing, but Amerla had never been one to shy away from uncomfortable truths. She could not even recall Belania's face or voice clearly now. Was she still in love with the woman she had married? She loved: of that she had no doubts, but was she in love still? How could she be when she no longer knew Belania, when she no longer remembered even her face?

Even strangers could be loved, but was it possible to be in love with a stranger? Amerla wasn't sure. What about her parents and Belania's? How would they feel? Would anyone even be happy to have her back? They probably believed her dead, and they must be used to their lives without her. Would there be a place for her there now? Would she even fit in anymore?

She felt her feet dragging the closer she got home. The people on the street barely paid her any attention. There were a few faces that looked familiar, but she could not recall who they were. There was a time she would have walked up to them and told them who she was and asked for their names, apologising for forgetting, but that Amerla was no more. The years with only Pelthiel and later the others had buried that part of her.

Pelthiel. Her heart clenched painfully. It wasn't fair that he should be trapped there, unable to leave. But then it wasn't fair that she had been trapped there either.

*He did it to protect me.*

Perhaps. But would her parents, would Belania, have just stood there and allowed her to be sacrificed to Utfer?

*None of them stopped me when I went on my mission. They had been happy to let me go.*

She swallowed down the bile that had risen to her throat. She could say it was different, but was it? They had known it was dangerous, just as she had, and yet, they had been proud and happy to see her go. Even Belania.

Chosen of the Gods.

Was there a worse mockery? Everyone had assumed that because she was chosen, she would win. After all, it was the Gods who had selected her to be their champion. To be their fucking puppet, to kill a man who had only wanted to be left alone.

Disgust filled her. She had listened to them, had believed them, had trusted them. All it had done was keep her away from everyone she had loved for eleven years.

But if they hadn't tricked her, she would never have met Kiriel or Sivreth or Heldith. Or Pelthiel.

Heldith. Her heart ached for him. It had been obvious that his feelings for Pelthiel were different from what they all had felt. Even when he was siding with Kiriel and trying to justify the Gods, he had been conflicted. He had done a good job of hiding it, but it had been there.

Sivreth. He had never openly said anything, but she had seen the scars on his body, scars that were not caused by battles. Besides, there were no longer frequent battles anywhere. Now he had to go back to that place again. She could only hope that since he was an adult now, he would at least be able to protect himself.

She stopped, her mouth dry and heart hammering, the thread of her thoughts lost. Belania was standing on the street, talking to two people. How had she ever thought she had forgotten her? The curve of her lips as she smiled, the way she pushed back a strand of hair from her cheek, the lilt of her laugh: it all came rushing back. She had changed too, physically. Her body was fuller, and there was a confidence about the way she held herself. She had always been self-conscious about her height, hunching in on herself, but now she held herself straight. Amerla felt her vision blur. She drew in a breath.

One of the people talking to Belania placed a hand on her stomach and Amerla's breath caught. That explained the fullness of her body, her posture. The softness of her features, the tenderness of her smile. Amerla turned around, chest heaving. She had allowed herself to hope; the Gods had threatened Belania and Amerla had let herself have something she had steadfastly refused to entertain for all these years.

She couldn't blame Belania. It had been eleven years, after all. It only needed five for Belania to be a free woman. She swallowed around the lump in her throat. Her parents' house was at the other end of the street. She could go there, but she had no faith that she could keep her eyes away from the woman who had been her wife once.

Belania was not likely to recognise her now, was she? She turned around, keeping her eyes riveted on the ground, drawing deep breaths. She took a couple of steps and stopped.

*What if I leave?*

Belania believed her dead. Probably her parents did too. Probably they all had moved on. If she went home now... how long before her anger and heartbreak drove her from here? How fair was that to her parents?

Amerla lifted her eyes to look at Belania, smiling and talking, and she blinked back the tears that had risen to her eyes. Amerla hadn't cried in years. She was not going to start now.

She turned away and walked back to the harbour. She could find passage on a ship. Amerla knew that her magic and skills would be useful. Most captains would take her on board for free in return for keeping the weather fair. Not that she needed the free board. She had the pouch of coins Pelthiel had given her. But she didn't want to be a passenger. She needed to work, and she had never been trained for anything except in warfare and magic.

A mage who could hold her own in battle was still valuable on a ship. She could also be as far away as she needed to be. She did not look behind her as she made her way back to the harbour.

# THIRTY FIVE

The door opened with a creak and the two people in the room looked up anxiously, but their faces fell immediately. Ryr hated this, hated that Heldith's parents still waited for him. It had been almost two years. The logical part of Ryr had accepted that his friend would not come back, but not every part of him was logical.

"How are you two doing?" he asked, more brightly than he felt. He had to try to cheer them up. "I'm going to the Southern Isles tomorrow. Perhaps we'll find some clue there."

"Ryrthin," Sorodin said. "You have been searching for him for months now. Perhaps it is time you stopped."

"I can't do that," Ryr said quietly.

"Why not?" Felithia asked. "Even we have accepted Heldith is lost. Why can't you? Give this up, Ryrthin. You have to live your life!"

Ryr could feel his throat closing up, and he swallowed. It was so good of them to try to do this because they felt he was wasting his life. But he had seen the hopeful expression on their faces when he had opened the door. They hadn't given up on

Heldith any more than he had.

"I can't give up because he would never have given up on me," Ryr said.

"Ryr, you can't spend your entire life looking for him," Sorodin protested.

"It's my life," Ryr said. "It's my choice what to do with it."

Sorodin gave him a hug.

"Thank you," he said. "I can't tell you how much it means to us, but Ryrthin, you're as important to us as Heldith is, and ... we just want you to have a life other than this endless search."

"It will end when I find him," Ryr said.

Heldith had been more than a friend. They had been brothers in all but blood, and Ryr was never going to stop looking. Heldith was alive somewhere. He was certain of that. Ryr was not ready to even think of any other possibility.

*He has to be alive!*

"I have to get the supplies ready for the voyage tomorrow," he said. "I just came to tell you I was leaving."

Sorodin and Felithia still looked utterly devastated, but they nodded. Ryr left the house and exited on to the familiar street. He could feel his vision blurring as he gazed down at it. He didn't even have to remember for memories to hit him. Heldith and he playing on this street, fighting each other and other friends, racing down the street, laughing.

He swallowed around the lump in his throat as he made his way to his own home. His father was sitting in front, on a stool, already drunk. He stared blearily at Ryr as he opened the door.

"Where were you?" he asked, his voice slurring.

"At Heldith's," Ryr said briefly.

He tried his best to make excuses for his father. The man

ad been like this since Ryr's mother had died, and that had been
o long ago that Ryr had to strain to remember what she had
ooked like. It had been Sorodin and Felithia who had taken care
of him while his father had spiralled into grief and drinks. As
much as he tried to tell himself that his father was like this
because of grief, he could never dredge up any remnant of
ffection or respect for the man.

"Why are you always there?" his father demanded. "Are
ou going away again?"

"I have to find Heldith," Ryr said. "I've already paid
Athian and Sevila. They'll bring you your food and medicines.
Asvia will come and clean the house once a day and wash your
lothes."

Even though Ryr never paid the tavern nor gave his father
any money, somehow his father had always managed to be drunk
out of his mind at all times. Ryr would do what he could to keep
his father fed and clothed in his absence, but he felt nothing for
the man. Years of neglect and drinking on his father's part had
burned away whatever affection Ryr must have had for him at one
time.

He checked that his clothes were all packed and that his
weapons were sharpened and free of rust. To keep them so during
the long sea voyage was a challenge, but by now Ryr had become
adept at it. He hefted his pack and his weapons. He would get
them on board the ship first. Falith would get provisions and
Bisthia would arrange for clean water. Ryr had to get medicines
as well as the charms to protect them from storms and sickness.

His father was still grumbling when Ryr left the house,
but he paid no attention to him. His father never even talked to
him except to complain about one thing or another. It no longer
bothered him, but he wasn't interested in listening to it either.

"Ryr!" Bisthia was running towards him, her dark hair

189

flying behind her. "Ryr! It's Heldith! He's back!"

Ryr stared at her, his mind and body both refusing to move for an instant, but only for an instant. He dropped his pack and sprinted towards the harbour, only one thought in his head. Heldith was back! He stopped only when he reached the edge of the wharf where Heldith was being helped on to the shore by a hard-faced young man, a few years older than them. He was a warrior, as was clear from the muscled and scarred body as well as the way he stood and moved.

"Heldith," Ryr said, his eyes drinking in the sight of his friend.

Heldith looked haggard, he had a beard that was overgrown, and his hair was also longer than usual and matted. He looked at Ryr and smiled, warmth radiating from it, and Ryr could see his friend again.

"Ryr," he said, and Ryr moved forward, enveloping his friend in his arms, holding him tight.

The man who had helped him said, "I'll be leaving, Heldith. Take care of yourself."

Heldith turned his head to the man. "Thank you, Sivreth. You too."

His voice broke slightly.

Ryr had questions, but he could not think of a single thing to say or ask as Heldith slumped against him, his face buried in his shoulder, and his frame started shaking with silent sobs.

# THIRTY SIX

*I* *have missed this.*

That was all Heldith could think as he clung to Ryr with everything, as he sobbed his heart out. It was more than joy and relief at seeing Ryr, of being back home. It was also the knowledge that he would never ever see Pel again.

*Why do I even want to see him now?*

Pelthiel had always been beyond him, had never been his in any sense of the word. He had always kept himself aloof, apart from them, except when they had forced a truth spell on him and–

It was too late to have regrets now. Heldith had been a fool, and the days that they spent at sea had made him see that more clearer than ever. Had he thought he could change the Gods' minds by making them see the truth? If it was that easy, the Gods wouldn't be who they were. In the end, all he had done was violate Pel's mind and make the man mistrust him completely. He might have laid bare Zeityl's betrayal of Pel, but that was not going to change the Gods' mind about either of them.

Besides, Heldith knew human nature. He hadn't lived very

191

long, but he had read books, and Pel had a library that would be the envy of any scholar. The Gods' natures weren't all that different from that of humans', and Zeityl was their blind spot. Zeityl whose memories still beat against a part of Heldith's own mind. He hated that he had them, the regret and the love the God had for Pel.

Pel, not Pelthiel. Pelthiel was what Zeityl thought of him as, and sometimes Heldith didn't know if the longing that coursed through him was his own or Zeityl's.

"Heldith," Ryr shook his shoulder. "Are you all right? You seemed far away all of a sudden."

Heldith looked around him to see that the tavern had almost emptied. He and Ryr had come in to have a drink, celebrating his return, and since Ryr hated alcohol, it had been a sacrifice on his part. The glasses of wine stayed untouched on their table, it was dark out, and the few guttering candles on their holders provided very little light.

"How long was I out for?" he asked.

Ryr looked anxious. "I've been shaking you and calling your name for almost an hour now. What's going on, Heldith?"

Heldith frowned. "I don't know," he said. "It's never happened to me before."

He was worried. He had thought he was thinking, but apparently something had caused him to black out. The empty space in his mind where the memory of the last few hours should have been concerned him. What was he even supposed to do now? What if this happened again? If it did, could Heldith be certain that he might be able to wake up?

He was aware of the gazes of the few patrons who remained in the tavern, and the muted whispers. The owner of the tavern was also looking at them with barely concealed curiosity.

"Let's go home," he told Ryr, and his friend nodded.

Outside, it was balmy, and they both walked side by side, steps firm and steady.

"Has that happened before?" Ryr asked.

Heldith shook his head. "No," he said. "I wasn't even aware that I had been spacing out for so long. I was thinking, but it didn't seem like it had been long."

"What was it that you were thinking about?" Ryr asked, his tone gentle. "The island?"

Heldith nodded, not knowing what else to say. He hadn't told anyone about Pel or Zeityl or the Gods. What was he to say? Pel was guilty of destroying Nagir, but it only bothered the Gods because it destroyed Utfer's powers. The lives lost meant nothing to them. Pel regretted it every day, and he had hidden himself away from the world and everyone because of that.

Then there was Zeityl, and how was he to explain that? He wondered if his spacing out for so long had something to do with Zeityl's memories at the back of his head. But there was no way he could be certain.

"Heldith," Ryr asked, his voice again soft. "You never speak of your time there. Did you suffer a lot?"

Heldith was startled. "No! Of course not!"

"Then, are you missing your days there? I can see that you're not happy, Hel. I just don't know why."

Heldith looked down. "I don't want to talk about it, Ryr."

Ryr nodded. "It's okay," he said. "You don't have to... just... you're not alone, Hel. I'm here, even if you don't want to talk."

Heldith nodded, his throat closing and chest tightening with emotion.

# THIRTY SEVEN

Lamier bowed out of the mayor's office, straightening once outside, and looking towards the closed door of the bedroom just opposite. The mayor's wife had locked her husband out of their shared bedroom since the death of their younger son. Lamier thought it a pity that she hadn't developed a spine while the child was alive.

Everyone said it was an accident, but Lamier had no doubt that Fedytiel had jumped off that cliff himself. He wished he had been able to protect the child. But he had not been able to protect Sivreth or Fedytiel, too afraid of the mayor and his violent temper.

*May the Gods forgive me.*

He had watched the mayor abuse his children and done nothing. When Sivreth was there, he used to protect his brother, and he had asked both his mother and Lamier to protect him when he had to leave.

Yet, both of them had been cowards, and only when she had nothing more to lose, had his lady developed a backbone. It was no use thinking about it now. How could he blame her when he himself had been such a coward? Of everyone, he was the one who knew her and all that she had to bear the best.

He knocked at the door to her room. "Madam? It is me, Lamier."

He felt the rush of magic as the door opened. Ah, so that was how she ensured her husband wouldn't gain entry to her room. He was not above forcing himself in, but physical strength was no match for magic. Lamier felt relieved. It would be a pity if the mayor's anger led him to harm his wife as well. Not that he hadn't done so. Lamier still remembered the two miscarriages as well as the broken bones, the bruises, and the many, many times that he had to use his own magic to heal her, since hers was inadequate.

"I dreamt of Sivreth," she said as he opened the door, carefully closing it behind him, and adding his own ward and seal to keep it closed. "He asked me why I didn't keep Fedytiel safe, and I... why didn't I, Lamier? Why was I such a coward that I couldn't protect my own sons from that beast?"

"I'm sorry," Lamier said. It was all he could say. He had been her guard when she was a maiden, and had come with her to this land, determined to protect her as his master had bidden him. But he had failed to do so, and now, he didn't know how to comfort her.

"Sometimes, I dream of them both," she whispered. "They ask me why I ever gave birth to them... why I didn't kill them in the womb itself so they wouldn't have had to suffer so much... Lamier, why is it that man is alive and well, and my sons aren't? Why is there no law that can punish him while I must endure in silence?"

"I don't know, madam," he replied. "I'm sorry."

Lamier had always been a coward of sorts, but he couldn't bear to see her pain. He had contemplated killing the mayor several times, but had stopped himself because of her and her children. Because he had mistakenly thought that they would suffer far more without that monster.

"If killing him would ease your pain even a bit, I would be happy to do it, madam."

She looked at him, something almost desperate in her eyes. "If you do that, you will have done me a favour that even the Gods cannot," she said. "And I will do anything I can to repay you, Lamier, to protect you."

Lamier would have liked to stab the mayor in the heart, to watch the life go out of his eyes slowly, but not if the lady wanted to protect him. He knew her, and she was not above admitting to it if that would help him. Poison would have to do.

"Madam," he said. "There would be no need of repayment or protection. I will do this and no one will know he's been murdered."

Lamier had been illiterate at one time, but Sivreth had taught him to read and write. Lamier was certain that he would be able to imitate the mayor's handwriting. A letter of remorse and death by poison would be all that was needed.

There was a knock on the front door, one that was soft, but insistent. Lamier looked at the closed door of the mayor's study and was glad to see that it stayed closed. He bowed to his lady.

"I will see who is at the door, Madam," he said. But before he could leave, one of the new servants had already opened the door.

# THIRTY EIGHT

The beating of his heart was too frantic, but Sivreth tried to breathe normally through it. He couldn't panic, not now. Not after everything he had been through. He had faced Gods, and a man more powerful than them, and he was here. What could his parents do to him after that?

To be fair, it was his father who had been abusive but his mother... well, she had never done anything to protect him or Fedytiel. Sivreth blamed her as much as he blamed his father. Still, he was an adult now, had been gone long enough, and had changed a lot as well. He didn't care that his father was the mayor and that he had the law on his side. If he tried to hurt him or Fedytiel again, he would fight back. Take Fedytiel and go somewhere. He would protect his brother.

For all that, he nearly felt dizzy as he saw the familiar building, right in the centre of the city. The house of the mayor. He swallowed hard. It had been years, and he wasn't sure what to expect any more. If not for Fedytiel, he would never have returned. But he couldn't leave his brother to face alone the hell he must have been in the last few years without Sivreth. It was the thought of Fedytiel that had been most prominent in his mind when he had been trapped on Pelthiel's island.

Would anyone even recognise him? Sivreth hoped not. It had been five years, after all. It had been Pelthiel who had kept track of the years, not any of them. For them, the days were all jumbled together into a mass of days and nights, but not to Pelthiel. Would he be all right, trapped on the island with his worst enemies? Would Zeityl's sacrifice be enough to keep him safe? Sivreth hoped so. He hated having to leave. It was only the thought of Fedytiel that had made it easier.

Sivreth swallowed hard, as he knocked on the door, scratching the beard he had not bothered to shave off. He knew he looked completely different now. His parents would have thought him dead. He would meet Fedytiel and no one else. How old would he be now? Twelve? Thirteen? He was nearing eight when Sivreth had left. He had to think for a moment to bring up his brother's face. Back on the island, everything about his past life had seemed unreal, like a bad dream he had woken up from.

An unfamiliar servant opened the door.

"Yes?" the woman asked, her face as impassive as if carved from wood.

"Is this Mayor Girodin's residence?" he asked, just to be certain.

"It is, sir. Do you have an appointment with the mayor?"

"Um, no. I wished to meet with Master Fedytiel."

His heart was in his mouth as he spoke. What lie could he tell in order to convince her to let him meet Fedytiel alone?

The woman's wooden face fractured, crumbled, and an expression of anguish replaced it.

"I'm sorry, sir," she said. "Master Fedytiel died in an

accident last year."

Sivreth marvelled at how steady his voice was as he spoke, "My condolences to the mayor and his wife. What happened?"

"He fell off the cliffs off the coast," she said, tears glittering in her eyes and her voice trembling.. "He used to play there."

"Fell," he said flatly.

Fedytiel had been afraid of heights, or at least he used to be. He would never go near the edge, even to play. He had always been careful like that when Sivreth last knew him.

And yet, why should this woman be lying? She seemed to genuinely care for Fedytiel.

The Gods had threatened to hurt Fedytiel. They must have known he was dead and yet, they had threatened him. There was a bitter taste in Sivreth's mouth, and he swallowed hard.

"I'm sorry," he said again.

"Who is it, Abrithia?" his father's voice could be heard, and Sivreth's head snapped to stare behind the woman. His father was not visible yet, but Sivreth's heart was hammering in his chest.

"I should be leaving," he said, keeping his voice steady. "I'm sorry about the boy."

He all but ran from there, only wanting to escape, not wanting to see the man again.

What now?

He hadn't even wanted to come back. Not here. He had never missed it, had never been safe or happy. He had loved his brother, and had fretted about him, but to be honest, he was glad to be spared the beatings, and the whippings, and the verbal lashings that had cut even more deeply at one time.

This had never been home.

Sivreth stopped in front of the largest inn in town.

Pelthiel had given them all enough money, so he could afford room and board. He needed a quiet place where he could think, to deal with this, and to decide what to do. He tried not to think of anything as he stepped inside.

"What can I do for you?" asked the pleasant-faced young man manning a curved wooden desk on the left.

The room only had the desk and a couple of couches and a short table. There was a door opposite the desk that led to the common room, and he could hear raucous laughter from within. There was a flight of stairs opposite where he stood and another door set on its right, and a corridor on its left. The whole place was clean, and the walls were painted in muted yellow.

"I need a room and food to be sent to my room immediately," he said, moving towards the desk. The young man looked faintly familiar, but Sivreth couldn't place him at all. "Are you a local here?"

The young man gave him a hard eyed stare this time. "That will be eleven feltins," he said.

Sivreth counted out fifteen coins and set them down on the desk. "I would need some hot water for a bath and for shaving."

"That's included in the price of the room," the man said, taking only the eleven coins.

"Do you have a name?" Sivreth asked.

"Firthil," the man said.

It was with an effort that Sivreth stopped himself from gasping. Firthil had changed. He didn't want to gape at the man, and he looked away. He heard a bell ring. Firthil must have pulled a bell rope. A large man appeared. Sivreth had no difficulty recognising this one.

Firthil slid a key across the desk.

"Room 104," he said. "Please follow Hevisthen. He'll also

bring your water and food."

"Bag," Hevisthen said, indicating the bag that was slung on Sivreth's shoulders.

"I'll carry it," Sivreth said, trying to stop his heart from racing as he followed Hevisthen.

It was as he closed the door behind Hevisthen that he realised that Firthil hadn't asked for his name.

# THIRTY NINE

On some days, Pel felt it was easy to go on living. But on others, it felt like a chain around his neck a weight that was so indescribably heavy. He dreamed of his sister, of his mother, of Heldith, of Zeityl, of Sivreth and Kiriel and Amerla, of the people who had come before him.

He had nightmares of Nagir, of lighting and fire, and his own fury, striking them without mercy, without thought.

Once Pel had thought he had lost control, but these days, he no longer thought or believed that. He might not have made a conscious choice, but at that point, there had been so much hatred in him, hatred for the Gods, for Zeityl and for the people of Nagir. He had wanted Nagir to be destroyed, to be razed to the ground, and for all the fanatic followers of Utfer to be killed. A part of him had even wanted to prove that the protection of the Gods meant nothing.

In the end, all his magic did was to do his bidding, no matter how unconscious. Pel might not have accepted it in the past, but he had still come to this island, and had chosen to sequester himself here. He had still wanted to stay away from the world, not out of fear, but out of grief and guilt. He didn't want the Gods to find him again, to repeat the tragedies of the past.

But apparently, the Gods hadn't been ready to let go. Because of Zeityl's sacrifice, they had been unable to even find him, but humans could. The compass was a useless thing, but in the hands of a human wielding magic, it could lead them wherever they wanted to go, and since they had wanted to find Pel, it had led them here.

"Serityl," he said softly, sinking down on his knees on the beach. "How is he?"

He no longer knew if he meant Zeityl or Heldith.

"He is fine," she said. "Sorrowful at his separation from you. Sad that you are trapped here, that his sacrifice had led to you being a prisoner."

Pel bowed his head. Destiny and destruction. The prophecy that his father had made Zeityl forget since he feared for Pel and his future. And yet, it had come true. Pel was Zeityl's destiny, and he became his ruin as well.

"He and I were never meant to be," Pel said, his heart aching. "And it is not his fault that I chose this... Tell him to be at peace."

"He will have peace when you are happy," she said softly. "And so will I."

Pel wanted to cry, but he could only smile, his vision blurring and chest tightening.

"I'll try," he said.

He wished it was that easy. His heart felt like it was going to shatter at any moment, as if everything that he was, was not real, as if his every breath, every movement, caused nothing but pain.

*Is this love? How can it be? Love isn't supposed to hurt*

203

*like this, is it?*

Pel bowed his head again, and let his tears fall, Serityl's waves lapping his knees and feet, as if trying to comfort him as the sound of his sobs were swallowed by her own soothing noises.

# FORTY

The ocean was quiet today. Not that it had ever been violent. Never in his life could Heldith remember it being anything but placid. The first time he had an inkling of just how rough the seas could be was when he had left home for Pel's island. The waves that rose many times above his head, and his sturdy boat, had seemed so small and fragile before them. The grey of the sky, and the churning waters around him, the lash of spray on his face, the wind buffeting the sails, and Heldith had never enjoyed a journey more.

He had never been afraid of the waters, and he certainly wasn't then. But now... his sojourn in Pel's island had changed him in more than one sense. It wasn't just the strange memories rattling around in his head, it wasn't just the way his heart felt like it couldn't beat again, it was the bone deep fear he felt for the ocean. He was afraid to even wet his feet at the beach. He didn't want her to touch him.

*Serityl, how long before your revenge is complete?*

And yet, she had let Zeityl do this, allowed a part of him to escape, allowed him this life and a chance to see Pel again. She had allowed him to come home.

*What magic does Pel have that she would do this for him?*

"Hel," Ryr's voice broke into his thoughts.

Heldith turned to look at his friend. Ryr stood just beyond the beach, head cocked to a side, eyes shadowed with concern. Heldith gave him a small smile as he made his way to his friend.

"How long have you been there?" he asked.

Ryr shrugged. "Long enough. You seemed lost in thought."

Heldith's eyes strayed back to the ocean. Would she let him go back to Pel ever again? Or did he have to sacrifice himself again?

He shook his head slightly, as if to get his mind off that thought.

"Are you all right, Hel?" Ryr asked.

"Yes," the lie sprang so easily to his lips. "Why do you ask?"

"Hel," Ryr said softly. "You're shitty at lying. Do you know that?"

Heldith swallowed. He should have known better than to lie to Ryr. He knew him better than he knew himself. Or at least, better than he used to know himself. Now... now, Heldith wasn't even sure who he was.

*Don't you mean what?*

Ryr sighed from beside him. "Hel," he said. "I'm not pushing you to tell me anything, but... you don't have to pretend with me. I know you, and I can see you're..." He sighed again. "You're like a man who has nothing left to live for, and I don't know what made you like this, I don't know what happened to you, and what you've been through. I get it if you don't want to talk about it, but Hel, I just want you to know that I'm here for you. You don't have to tell me anything, but I'm here if you want a shoulder to lean on."

Heldith gave him a small smile. "That's quite a speech," he said lightly, turning his face away so Ryr wouldn't see the tears that had risen to his eyes. "Been practicing it?"

"Don't be facetious," Ryr said, but his tone was light too.

It would be a relief to tell Ryr everything, to get everything off his chest, but what could he tell? That he was sort of a reincarnation of a God? Even Ryr was not going to believe that. He could say he had fallen for Pel, but... but had he? Was it Zeityl's emotions, or was it his? How could he be certain? He might be a part of Zeityl reborn, but he was also Heldith, and he had a mind of his own, thoughts of his own.

If that was so, and if it was because of Zeityl that he had fallen for Pel, there was no reason for him to feel as if he could never smile again.

His feelings for Pel were something he didn't want to talk about. Not because he didn't think Ryr wouldn't understand, but because he didn't want sympathy or understanding or compassion. It had been his own fault. He couldn't blame Pel for how he had sent him away. Would he have forgiven someone for it? Zeityl had betrayed him, too. It was as if no matter who he took life as, he was destined to do this, to hurt Pel, to do things no one could or should forgive.

"It was all a lie," he said finally, his throat tight and chest constricting. "The Gods... they lied... the mission, being chosen... it was all just a manipulation."

Ryr said nothing for a moment.

"I'm not doubting you," he spoke slowly. "But they're Gods, Hel. Why would they do something like that?"

*Because they're idiots who are blinded by revenge.*

But how could he even be angry when he understood the

love behind that revenge? Their mistake was in going after Pel in the first place, in what they had done to his father, and Leithia. For a moment, Heldith was unable to breathe; something was burning inside him, almost like someone was twisting a heated knife into his heart and turning it excruciatingly slowly.

"They're all-powerful," Ryr was continuing. "What have they to gain by manipulating a human?"

"If they're that powerful, why do they need a human to kill someone?" Heldith asked.

"They chose you," Ryr said. "Perhaps this is all a test. Perhaps that's why they gave you this task. To test you."

"Well, I failed," Heldith said baldly. "Spectacularly too. Neither my magic nor my skills were any match for him."

Ryr gave him a sharp glance.

"If the Gods want him dead, they would find a way," he said, and for a moment Heldith felt dizzy before it struck him that Ryr was trying to comfort him. He probably thought Heldith hated the man he had been sent to kill and had failed. The knife inside his heart had stilled, been drawn out and been plunged in again.

"Hel," Ryr said again. "What's wrong?"

Heldith shook his head, dredging up a smile. How could he tell Ryr that his words had caused this reaction? That it had caused his insides to twist and for his chest to tighten?

"We should go home," Heldith muttered, his eyes still staring out at sea. What if Ryr was right? Pel was as trapped as the Gods. What if the Gods found a way to kill him?

*They can't while they are on the island, not when Pel is protected by Zeityl's sacrifice.*

But what if they took the chance? Revenge was a powerful motivator, after all.

Heldith wanted to run into the ocean, to make his way to

the island. Except he couldn't. Now that he remembered part of who he was, Serityl would never let him cross her. If he attempted now, she would take him and this time, there would be no Pel to save him, and no escape from her hold.

Ryr's hand was on his shoulder, warm and comforting, and Heldith drew in a deep breath. It was no use wishing. He was here now, and he had no way of making it back to Pel. He turned from the sea and smiled at his friend.

"I'm fine," he said.

No matter how many times he said it, it would never be true, but perhaps he could ease the minds of those around him.

# FORTY ONE

K iriel didn't know what he was doing any longer. He felt out of place in his village, in his home. His sister's eyes were guarded, and though his mother was happy to have him, he couldn't pretend that there wasn't a shadow in her eyes whenever she looked at him. Guilt and grief warred within his chest, though the logical part of him chided him for the remorse. His father had made the choice to stay. It wasn't as if Kiriel had forced him. But the regret wouldn't leave.

The girl he had loved once was married now, but somehow Kiriel wasn't bothered by it. It was not as if he hadn't expected it, after all. He didn't think he would have fit into her life any more in any case. There were too many things inside him, too much betrayal, too much grief, too much guilt, too much *stupidity.*

How could he have trusted the Gods so blindly? How could he have been so blind as to not see that Pelthiel was a good man? Not that it would have made any difference, but up until the night they had forced a truth spell on Pelthiel, he had had some hopes that he had at least been doing the right thing, that whatever he lost, it was because he had no choice. Since that night, even that comfort was denied him. The Gods wanted revenge, and his life, their lives, were the price. They mattered nothing.

*And I was foolish enough to fall for that.*

Yet, he had thought of attacking Pelthiel. When the Gods had threatened his family, his sister, he had been ready to sacrifice Pelthiel. If not for Heldith, they might well have killed him that night, because somehow Kiriel knew that Pelthiel wouldn't have fought back, not against the threat that the Gods held above them.

Heldith saved his life, and Pelthiel still kicked him out.

Pelthiel might have sacrificed himself for them in the end—for no matter how he put it, it was a sacrifice to allow himself to be trapped in a place with his worst enemies as the only company—but that didn't mean what he did to Heldith wasn't cruel.

Kiriel missed Heldith, Sivreth and Amerla, and even Pelthiel. He had belonged there, on the island. He no longer did here.

*I just need time to get used to being here.*

He wished he could believe that.

Kiriel wandered the streets of his town, reacquainting himself with the place. He sauntered into the woods, trying to reawaken memories of his childhood. His old friends were still there, and reconnecting with them had been easy on the surface, but Kiriel could feel the wrongness of it all. He was something that didn't fit among them anymore. He wanted to, and he tried. A week passed and two, and still he felt as if he was a stranger here.

"Are you planning to leave?" Aderla asked one evening.

He stared at her. He had no plans, and for all his feeling

out of place, he was still trying.

"Why should I?" he asked, forcing a smile. "I'm home."

"If you had been home when you were supposed to, father would be alive," she said, her eyes as harsh as her words, merciless and precise.

His breath stopped. "You speak as if I stayed away by choice," he said when he could find words again.

"It doesn't really matter, does it?" Her eyes were shimmering now, though her words were hard. "You weren't here, and he chose to stay because he was waiting for you." A sob escaped her throat. "He died, waiting for you to come home, and you... you aren't even happy to be here!"

Kiriel wanted to refute that accusation, but the words wouldn't come. He wasn't happy. He couldn't even pretend to be.

"How do you expect me to be happy when he isn't here?" he asked, giving back cruelty for cruelty, hurt for hurt. "You may have got used to his absence and his death, but it is fresh to me."

Her lips drew back in a snarl, and she was equally malicious as she said, "You spent years without any of us. Don't pretend like you aren't used to his absence."

The door opened, and Kiriel turned away from his sister and smiled at his mother. It was easy to smile at her, because despite the shadow that lay in her eyes, her smile was bright enough to rival the sun when she saw him. He wanted to belong, to try, to make a place for himself here, for her sake. But he doubted if he would be able to. Harsh, she might have been, but Aderla was right. He was unhappy, and it wasn't just his father's death that had caused it.

He went to bed early, but lay awake, and when the tiny knock came at his door, he knew who it was.

"I'm sorry," Aderla said as she entered his room, padding silently to his side. "I... I thought you were leaving.... I want you to stay."

He couldn't speak, couldn't reassure her, couldn't even offer an apology in return, and she gazed at him for a moment before leaving the room. In his nightmares, he killed his father and Pelthiel and Heldith sat on the sandy beach, looking at him with hollow eyes.

"Kiriel," a familiar voice was in his dream, and Kiriel's fury knew no bounds.

"Get out of my head and stay out!" he told the God.

"I chose you for a reason," Amythia said, her voice soft and warm, and her eyes glowing.

An expletive burst from his lips and he woke with an effort of will, his heart hammering and his mouth dry. Of course, the Gods could still send them visions. Honestly, what were they expecting? Were they expecting him to be their puppet again, to listen to their lies again? He lay back down again, but sleep remained in abeyance for the rest of the night.

# FORTY TWO

Amerla sat huddled in a corner of the boat. It had been a quick trip and tomorrow they would make port. Back home again. Her heart fluttered in her chest. What was home anymore? She was planning to find another boat and get a position. Perhaps this would be a longer trip. She could always hope.

She looked out at the sea. It lay calm, and the sight brought a wave of nostalgia.

*Great. Now, I'm missing my prison.*

It wasn't the island, though. It was Pelthiel, and Kiriel and Sivreth and Heldith. Somehow, insensibly, they had become family to her. Of course, she wouldn't be missing them this much if she wasn't so unmoored. She was honest enough to know that the loss of her real family was the reason she was thinking of them so often.

*I can go home to my parents. No one's stopping me.*

She could, but then she would need to see Belania again, and her new husband, and pretend to be happy for her and smile and go on as if everything was fine. That wasn't going to last if she knew herself. She would be driven to leave by her need not to see Belania again. It wasn't that she wasn't happy for Belania, or that she didn't want Belania to be happy. The fair part of her brain told her that she should be happy that Belania found someone, that she hadn't waited. But that was only a part of her. Most of her was hurt and grieving. It wasn't her fault that she couldn't come home after all.

She needed the distance now. Perhaps someday, she could handle this with grace, if not equanimity, and till that day came, it was better for her to stay away.

As the boat approached the harbour, her eyes started scanning the ships and boats moored there. None of them looked ready to depart within a day or two. She suppressed a sigh. There were inns where she could stay for a few days. She had enough money. But she would have liked to leave as quickly as possible. Perhaps she could go visit her friends. How was Sivreth faring? And Heldith? Would Kiriel had had better luck than her? Somehow, the thought only made her sad.

She made her way down the gangway, giving the captain a smile and accepting his words of gratitude. As soon as she was on land, she swayed a little. Damn, she needed food and a bed, but she needed to know which ships would leave first and if they needed a mage. She made her way to the harbourmaster's office. She knew one of the people there, the one who sat outside and had all the news about what ships were leaving when. Her next stop was the inn which the ship captains preferred. The captain of the *Chimera* was there, a large balding man with a potbelly and loads of facial hair.

"I heard you would set sail by the end of the week," she said.

He looked her over, his eyes narrowed. "We don't have room for passengers," he said. "We carry goods to the Southern Isles."

STOLEN FROM A DREAM

"I'm a mage," she said. "And a soldier. I would be happy to work in return for food and board."

He scratched his chin. "We have guards, but we would be happy to have a mage on board. You can work the weather?"

"I can."

He nodded. "You may have to share with the guards. We have no separate quarters for mages."

"That's all right," she said.

"All right. Be on the ship early on, four days hence. We sail with the first tide."

She nodded as she made her way out, her stomach growling loudly. There was a small inn at the edge of the harbour, which was more expensive than the others. It was also cleaner and the food and ale were better. She made her way to it, ignoring the crowd and the pull of her own heart that wanted her to go home.

She took a room and ordered food and also a bath. Now that she was here, she was glad for the four days' break. Her supply of clean clothes was limited. She had been using magic to clean them, but somehow they never felt clean to her. The stink of fish and cheap ale still clung to her clothes and body. Her skin felt encrusted with salt.

An hour later, she had bathed, changed and fed, and was contemplating the bed. It looked clean and inviting, but she had never been in the habit of napping during the day, not even while she was on the island and when it was only she and Pelthiel. She sat down on a chair instead and took out a torn tunic. There were sewing supplies in the room.

She set the stitches slowly. This wasn't work she was used to. She yawned, and the needle pricked her finger.

"Amerla."

She started, staring at the figure who stood in front of her. "How are you here?"

"You're dreaming," Hamithia said. "We forgive you for failing in your task, Amerla. We'll forgive all if you could just free us."

She laughed as she jabbed her hand with the needle. The pain jerked her awake. She looked around the room, her breath coming fast. It had been a dream, but it worried her. Why now? It had been almost two months since they had left. Why did the Gods suddenly decide to get help?

She bit her lip. If they could send dreams, what if they sent someone else? Another chosen? With the Gods helping them actively, they could even win.

*I have to warn Pelthiel.*

A knock came on her door.

# FORTY THREE

The days passed by quickly even though he had nothing to do, but Sivreth didn't grudge that. He needed the time. He wandered the town and if his steps took him to a certain cliff frequently, well, no one else needed to know that. No one in the town seemed to recognise him, and that was just how he preferred it. His worries about Firthil not asking him for his name were for naught. He had learned since that the inn had a policy of not asking people's names and details in order to protect their privacy.

It was strange seeing people who were familiar to him pass him on the street, no recognition on their faces. It was oddly freeing as well. Had four years wrought so much change in him? Sivreth scratched his chin absently. He had not shaved off his beard or moustache, letting them add another level of anonymity. He kept them trimmed, something he had not bothered with while on the island.

Thoughts of his friends intruded occasionally, and so did thoughts of Pelthiel. Honestly, Sivreth would have preferred to have stayed on the island. He had come only because of Fedytiel.

He put his hands in his tunic pocket and drew out the small object that he carried everywhere. It was a small golden compass that Pelthiel had given him before he had left. Sivreth stared at it, emotion suffocating him.

Going back to the island was an option he had frequently considered these past two weeks. But first he needed time, time to get used to his loss, to say goodbye, and somehow to leave this town, this cliff, seemed a betrayal of Fedytiel.

*He's gone.*

Sivreth didn't want to think of that. He had apologised to Fedytiel and cried and shouted at the Gods, but nothing was helping. He didn't think anything would. He was even angry at Pelthiel for keeping him on the island.

*If he hadn't, I would also be dead now.*

Besides, it wasn't as if he had even wanted to leave. In spite of his love for Fedytiel, he had been relieved that he didn't have to come back. Sivreth sighed as he put the compass back in his pocket and looked out to the sea. It would be so easy to go back, to stay on Pelthiel's island. He gave the ocean one more glance and turned to go, only to stop short as he came face to face with his father.

His brain stopped working, his heart raced in his chest, and his mouth was dry. If he had been capable of thought, he would have noticed his father's eyes held no recognition, but even though he saw it, it didn't register. Sivreth took a couple of hurried steps back. He saw his father's face change, become panicked, and his mouth open, but Sivreth could hear nothing. His feet found only air as he took another step back.

Sivreth dredged up enough strength to cast a spell that encased him in a bubble and turned him invisible as he floated down the cliff. Dammit! His father hadn't even recognised him, and he had acted like a complete idiot. Now, his father might get suspicious. After all, it was not reasonable behaviour even if he had been startled. People didn't blindly backtrack to the edge of a cliff in surprise.

The bubble settled on the sandy beach and Sivreth looked up to see his father standing on top of the cliff. From this far down, he couldn't make out his expression. He might be wondering where the stranger went. Sivreth cursed under his breath. He had used magic and his father would certainly notice. He was panting heavily, and it had nothing to do with magical exertion.

"Sivreth," a familiar voice spoke and Sivreth stilled, turning around. There was no one, but he had not imagined that voice.

"Sivreth," the voice was stronger this time and Sivreth stared at the ocean, frowning. Was the ocean speaking to him?

"Hello?" he said, tentative. "Who is it?"

A form rose above the waves, shimmering and transparent, like sea foam given form.

"Heldith?" Sivreth stared at the apparition.

"I'm Zeityl," it said. "Pelthiel is in danger. You must go to him. Take your friends as well. Especially Heldith. He needs to be there."

"Zeityl." His brain tried to recall where he had heard that name. "Who are you?"

"It's not important. If you don't hurry, it would be too late!"

It came to him then, where he had heard the name.

"You're a God," he said, taking a step back. "You're dead."

"Gods cannot die," Zeityl said. "But I've no time for explanations. Serityl has allowed me this reprieve to warn you. You must hurry!"

"Even if I hurry, I won't be reaching him in an instant," Sivreth said. "Especially if I have to collect everyone else."

"I shall help you," Zeityl said. "Who do you want to reach first?"

Sivreth considered. Kiriel was nearest, but he had a feeling that if they were in as much as a hurry as Zeityl thought, he would need Heldith first. His magic was the most powerful.

"Heldith," he said. "I need to get to Heldith."

The next instant, everything around him blurred: the ocean, Zeityl, the cliffs. They disappeared in the blink of an eye and reformed into completely unfamiliar surroundings.

"Sivreth?" Heldith's astonished glance was on him. "How did you get here? What are you doing here?"

They were on a beach, but there were no cliffs towering over, only golden sand and palm trees, and beyond, Sivreth could see a village. The ocean lay calm and clear, even the waves breaking on the shore seemed quiet. The breeze was warm, feeling like an embrace from a lover. Heldith stood on the beach with a man who looked vaguely familiar.

"Pelthiel is in danger," Sivreth said. "We need to go."

Heldith's face was pale, his eyes large as he stared at Sivreth. "How do you know?"

"I... I had a vision of sorts... Zeityl told me... he said we had to hurry. He brought me here."

The Gods were truly powerful if a dead God could do this. But hadn't Zeityl said he wasn't dead?

"Hel?" It was only then that Sivreth recollected where he had seen the other person. He was there at the port, the man into whose arms Heldith had stumbled into as soon as he touched the shore. "What is going on?"

"I need to go, Ryr," Heldith said.

Sivreth saw the confusion on the other man's face, but

there was also resignation there. Heldith's face, on the other hand, held a fierce determination.

The skies opened above them, suddenly and unexpectedly, drenching them in moments.

# FORTY FOUR

It was surreal what was happening; Heldith knew he should stop and think, question Sivreth, ask him more about Zeityl, but he couldn't think beyond the fact that Pelthiel might be in danger. He couldn't even stop to think of Ryr or his parents.

"How are we getting there?" he asked.

"We've got to get Amerla and Kiriel too, according to Zeityl." Sivreth replied.

He looked pale and gaunt, his cheeks were hollowed, and he had lost weight. Heldith wanted to ask what had happened to him, worry burgeoning in his mind, but perhaps it could wait.

"But how will we get them and get to Pelthiel in time?" he asked.

"Will either of you slow down?" Ryr growled. "Who is Zeityl? Who are you?" to Sivreth, "And who the fuck is this Pelthiel? Why in the name of all the Gods are you rushing to save him?"

"Ryr," Heldith sighed as he turned to his friend. "I'll tell you everything once I come back, I promise. But now, I've to go."

"And who'll tell your parents?" Ryr asked.

"Tell them, please." Heldith said. It wasn't fair to them or to Ryr and he knew it, but he didn't want to lose any more time. "Please?"

"Will you even be back?" Ryr asked.

Heldith frowned. "Of course. I promised, didn't I?"

Why was Ryr asking him that, and why did he look so sceptical? But he had no time to worry about that either.

"What do we do?" he asked Sivreth.

Sivreth pointed to the ocean and there on the waves was a shimmering form, a face as familiar to him as his own. It was his own face, but with so much majesty and wisdom etched into its lines. It was an ageless face, but Heldith could also see the suffering on it.

"You're in pain," he said.

"I've been suffering since I took the decision," Zeityl replied. "That is the price Serityl demanded. That is why your memories and powers are incomplete."

"Because you have to be there, to suffer," Heldith said.

"We have no time for all this," Zeityl said.

"Yes, we do," Heldith said, waving a hand. The entire universe stilled. The breeze died down, the waves stopped, Ryr and Sivreth were immobile.

*Time stopped. The fucking time stopped because I waved my hand!*

"I need to know," Heldith said. "I need to understand."

"You know what you fear isn't true," Zeityl said softly, an almost amused smile on his face. "You loved him before you even realised who you were. Your feelings for him are your own, and have nothing to do with me."

"But I can't discount the possibility that I fell for him because I have part of your soul," Heldith said. "That my choice s it was, wasn't predetermined."

"Your soul may have started from mine, but it is not ntirely mine," Zeityl said. "If it was, do you think my siblings vouldn't have recognised you?"

"People are good at seeing only what they want to see," Ieldith said drily. "And apparently Gods are too. If what you say s true, how is it that I can just wave my hand and stop time?"

"You have my powers, and they grow along with your wareness of your truth." Zeityl paused. "Ask yourself if you will, low you can wave your hand and stop time, but you couldn't lefeat Pelthiel?"

Heldith stared.

"Because of your sacrifice," he said slowly. "It wasn't just ecause of his power, because I was always more powerful... but it vas your power... and you would never harm him."

"I betrayed him and hurt him, and I lost him," Zeityl said oftly. "When Serityl offered me the chance for a part of me to be uman, I thought that perhaps you could have the chance I never lid."

"Well, I fucked up too. Guess Gods don't have a nonopoly on that." Heldith tried not to let his bitterness show. But this was Zeityl, and it was almost like pretending to himself.

"You don't know him if you believe that," Zeityl said oftly.

Heldith turned his head away, not wanting to see the truth n Zeityl's eyes, the truth that he had always known in the leepest parts of himself. It was not as if he could lie to himself, lot when he was two people and one of them could apparently ee into the other's soul.

"How is he in danger?" he asked.

"They still retain the power to visit people in dreams," Zeityl said softly. "And they've never hated him more."

225

Heldith ran a hand across his face.

"I'd hoped knowing what you sacrificed for him might change their minds."

"They wouldn't be who they are if their minds could be changed that easily," Zeityl said. "Besides, whatever you may have told them, by now they've convinced themselves that it was all just an elaborate plot engineered by Pelthiel."

There was something in the way Zeityl said Pel's name, something so indescribably fond, and it made tears start to Heldith's eyes and also made him want to rip Zeityl's tongue out for daring to utter Pel's name in that tone.

"Why can't you tell them?" Heldith demanded.

"They'll probably think I'm the result of some spell crafted by him too," Zeityl sounded sad and resigned.

"And you think my friends and I can protect Pel from whatever threat your siblings have created?" Heldith asked. He had to bite his tongue not to say, "our siblings."

"Understand this." Zeityl sounded forbidding. "Pelthiel is the most powerful human in the world. He can handle whatever threats they come up with. But we don't want another Nagir, do we?"

Heldith frowned. "Was that what happened in Nagir?"

"I cannot tell you," Zeityl said softly. "Either you will remember or he will tell you, but I cannot be the one to say it."

Heldith looked at Zeityl, a frown on his face. "You do know that I can see when you aren't being completely honest, don't you?"

It seemed their connection worked both ways.

Zeityl sighed. "I fear he may not want to save himself," he whispered. "Every person has a breaking point, and I fear Pelthiel may have reached his."

Heldith nodded. "All right. Now, am I powerful enough

to transport Sivreth or do I have to depend on you?"

"It is better to let me do it. You have the power, but better not to let anyone know that yet." Zeityl paused. "They're all very powerful, but I've always been the most powerful of them all... Even if they weren't powerless, their collective power would still only equal yours. Why do you think I was the one chosen to brave Serityl? None of them could have survived that journey intact."

Heldith stared at that.

"Now, restart time. I've told you all I can. We need to get going." Zeityl sounded impatient.

# FORTY FIVE

When he woke, Kiriel wasn't sure why it felt as if he had had no sleep at all. There was something niggling at the edge of his mind, but he couldn't recall it. He remembered his fight with Aderla and her apology perfectly.

He should apologise to her, tell her he wouldn't leave, but somehow he couldn't bring himself to say the words. He wasn't happy, but it wasn't her fault or his mother's or anyone else's. It had been too long, and he was like a piece of their lives that didn't fit anymore. No matter how hard they tried, neither he nor they could pretend that things were the same as it had been before he had left.

Jitya had moved on, had got married to someone else and had no thoughts left to spare for him. It seemed unfair that his sister and his mother couldn't do the same. His father had died due to his inability to move on, and now his mother and Aderla were trying to make Kiriel fit into their lives for his father's sake as much as their own. He was doing the same as well, no matter how hard he might try to resist it. The shadow of his father lay over them all.

Everything was quiet in the kitchen as Kiriel took his seat

at the dining table.

"How did you sleep?" his mother asked, ruffling his hair while Aderla served him breakfast in silence.

"I slept well, thank you," he said. "Aderla, when you are free, can we talk?"

Her face was pale, but she nodded, and their mother looked from one to the other. "What are you two up to?" she asked, a worried frown on her face.

"Just catching up." Kiriel gave his mother an easy smile. "I mean, I missed a lot of her life, so I thought it would be nice to spend some time together."

His mother nodded. "It must be strange," she said softly. "We're all strangers to you now."

"You'll never be a stranger," he said, hating how anxious she looked, how sad, how afraid, as if he would just up and leave again.

She placed a hand on his shoulder. "I don't blame you for anything," she said. "You talk to your sister. I'll be in the garden."

Kiriel pushed his food around, not hungry anymore. Aderla sat down next to him. "What do you want to talk about?"

"I want to tell you what happened," he said. "But I want you to promise that you won't tell anyone else."

She nodded. "I promise, but,"—she chewed her lower lip— "You don't have to tell me anything. If... if this is an apology, I don't want it... I... I started it, said things I shouldn't have... I was scared, and I tried to hurt you, and you don't owe me anything."

She bit her lip again as she looked down, but he could see the tears dripping down her face, though she did not sniffle or sob. Kiriel raised a hand to touch her shoulder and dropped it. He didn't know her well enough to know if it would be welcome. He might be her brother, but she was not a child anymore.

"I want to tell you," he said. "I need you to know."

229

She nodded. "All right."

He told her everything. About Pelthiel, Amerla, Sivreth, Heldith, about the Gods, the lying cheating Gods, about the days spent on the island, resentful and yet serene, about the bonds forged and friendships grown, about the truth spell, about the fight. By the time he ended it, his voice was hoarse. He did not look at her, and he did not cry in spite of how his eyes burned.

"Oh, Kiriel," she whispered. "I... I didn't know."

"I didn't tell you to make you feel bad," he whispered.

"I know," she said. "Do you... do you wish you were back there?"

Did he? He didn't know, and wasn't that scary?

"It was simple there," he said. "Easy... we only had boredom to contend with... memories, frustration, anger... they all drained away after a while... and the others... we... we were all we had, and..." He sighed. "I miss them." He ended.

They both fell silent and he could hear his mother humming to herself as she worked in the garden.

"Is this Kiriel's house?"

His head snapped up as he jumped to his feet. He knew that voice! He was moving to the door, wrenching it open even before his mother had finished answering, his heart thrumming.

"Sivreth! Heldith!"

He hugged them both, feeling insensibly happy.

"Good to see you, Kiriel," Heldith said.

"What are you doing here?" Kiriel's eyes scanned them both. They both looked as bad as he felt, but they were both uninjured as well, and till he saw that Sivreth was not sporting any new bruises, he hadn't even known how worried he had been

"Pelthiel is in danger," Heldith said. "We need to go. Now."

"Kiriel?" his mother asked, fear in her voice, and anxiety.

He turned to her and moved towards her, hugging her tight. "I'll come back. I promise. But I need to go now."

Her look on his face was searching and sorrowful, but she nodded. "You have to do what you should," she said.

He turned to look at Aderla, who was looking at him with a strange expression on her face.

"Aderla," he began, not knowing how to say goodbye to her just yet.

She forestalled him by stepping forward and hugging him. He hugged her back, his heart lighter than it had been since he had returned.

"Come back," she whispered. "Safely, if you can manage it."

He chuckled weakly. "I promise," he said, kissing her on top of her head. He turned to his friends. "How are we going?"

"We have some divine help," Sivreth said. "Zeityl."

"But I thought he was dead," Kiriel was confused.

"Not really, but no time to explain it all now. We need to get Amerla too," Heldith said.

Kiriel turned to his family one more time and gave them a soft smile.

"I'll see you soon," he said.

This time, he was certain of it.

# FORTY SIX

The knock was repeated, louder and Amerla wrenched open the door, an angry exclamation on her lips, but it died down as she saw the man standing outside. She recognised him as the man who had been with Belania, but there was something naggingly familiar about his face and his crooked smile.

"Amerla," he said, his smile widening, and she took a step back.

"Drelin!"

She was shocked, but happy to see him. Somehow, she couldn't even be angry at him. He had always been in love with Belania, even when they had been children. Besides, they all must have thought her dead. Belania couldn't have made a better choice.

He laughed as he stepped forward to sweep her into his arms, hugging her tight enough to bruise.

"It is you!" His voice was choked as well. "I couldn't believe it when I saw you at the harbourmaster's office. I thought I must be hallucinating." He took a step back, his arms still around her, as he looked at her. "You've changed, but not so much I wouldn't recognise you."

"Same," she said, giving him a mock punch on his arm.

"I don't understand," he said. "How long have you been back?"

She drew a deep breath. "Couple of months."

"Why didn't you come home?" he asked.

Finally, the question she had been dreading. She looked at his face, care and concern and confusion on his face. She could tell him the truth, that she had come home and had found Belania had moved on to him, but could she do that to him? Drelin had always been a friend, and there had been a time when she had dreamed of him as much as she had about Belania, but he'd never had eyes for anyone except Belania.

*I can't hurt either of them.*

She shrugged. "What do you want me to say? It has been over ten years... I just... I was afraid... I was storing up the courage."

"Afraid," he repeated. "Of what, Amerla?"

She broke from his hold and moved towards a window, staring out. "That you had all moved on, that Belania..." Her voice choked and broke, but she swallowed and continued. "That she may have found someone else... that my parents... everyone would be used to me not being there... I... I wasn't even sure if anyone would recognise me, if they would remember me."

"I don't..." She heard his sharp exhale. "I don't pretend to understand how you feel," he said quietly. "But I want you to know that you are not forgotten. You never will be. You are remembered, and you are loved just as much as you were when you left. By everyone."

"She didn't have to wait," Amerla said, both angry and disappointed in him for lying to her. Why was he even doing that? "I mean, I've been gone all this time, and she... she could have found someone else. I mean, no one would blame her if she did..."

"What about you?" he asked. "Would you blame her?"

She shook her head, still not looking at him. "No," she said. "I wouldn't. How can I? I might never have come back. How is it fair to expect her to wait?"

He was silent for such a long time that she wondered if he had left.

"Amerla," he said finally. "I married her. A couple of years ago."

It felt as if there was something inside her chest, stopping her from breathing. It felt as if someone had put their fist through her heart.

"I wish you both happiness," she said, her voice breaking in spite of herself and tears that she had held inside so far bursting forth.

"Amerla." He caught her by the shoulder, turning her around, and he was again holding her. "I'm sorry," he whispered. "I'm so sorry,"

"No," she choked out. "You... I'm happy for you both... I really am..."

"We aren't," he said, as he lifted her face and looked at her, a look of determination on his face. "We aren't, and we will never be. We miss you too much."

She stared at him, her mind feeling too sluggish and latching on to the only thing it could understand.

"We?"

"We," he said firmly. "You never had eyes for anyone except Belania, or you would have known how much I was in love with you."

She couldn't understand what he was saying. "I thought

you were in love with her," she said.

"I was in love with you both," he said, sighing. "And I still am, and she still loves you. That I know. Do you know that we named our unborn daughter after you? She's called Amerla."

Amerla stared at him, not comprehending what he was saying. "You both missed me?"

He nodded, and there was a look of determination and desperation on his face. "So, what I want to ask is if you'll marry me, so we can all be together?"

She broke away from his arms again.

"I... I need to think..."

What he was proposing was common enough, but she had never contemplated it, because she had never thought she could have it. Whatever infatuation she had on Drelin had sputtered out long ago.

"I'm not in love with you," she said finally. "If I accept, it will only be for her, and that's not really fair to you."

"I know you aren't in love with me," he said. "But I also know that you do love me. Perhaps it is only as a friend. But I'm ready to accept that. I hope it will change, but if it doesn't—" He shrugged. "Having any part of you is better than nothing. You've no idea how empty we've both been all these years."

Before she could answer, the door was flung open and three people rushed in. "Amerla!"

"Kiriel! Sivreth! Heldith! What are you doing here?"

"Pelthiel is in danger," Sivreth said. "We've to go to him now."

"No time to explain," Heldith said. "Please, Amerla, we need you."

Amerla looked at Drelin, who looked surprised and bewildered. She sighed. She couldn't let Pelthiel down.

"I've got to go," she said to him. "But I'll be back." She

paused. "And I agree. All right?"

His face was transformed with joy. "We'll be waiting."

She turned to her friends. "How are we getting there?"

# FORTY SEVEN

As he saw the approaching boats, Pel knew he should perhaps have expected this. The Gods would never change and their hatred of him was too virulent. What filled him with despair was seeing that the boats were once again full of *children*. Why did they always have to choose children? Pel held out a hand, whispering,

"Serityl, help me, please."

The ocean rose like a wall in front of the nearest boat, a wall of churning water between the boats and the island.

"You think that will stop them?" Ementiar asked from behind him.

Pel shrugged as he turned to face the Gods. They all stood there, facing him, faces full of glee and hate.

"It will slow them down enough," he said.

"Enough for what?" Brolar asked. "They are here because we asked them! They will listen only to us. They are not your brainwashed and misguided soldiers."

Pel started laughing. It was too exquisitely funny to hear the Gods accuse him of brainwashing and misguiding people.

"Stop laughing at us!" Keithia snarled. "How dare you,

mortal!"

At which Pel laughed harder.

"If we had our powers," growled Poltiel.

"But you don't," Pel said, turning back to the ocean, his mind back to the bleak despair of his thoughts.

The water wouldn't hold them back forever. Pel had no doubt that he could take them all on and win, but did he want to? The Gods would only keep bringing more and more people here. As long as they could still affect dreams, they were dangerous. That was what needed to stop.

Pel considered his course of action carefully. He could bind them, hold them on this island, powerless not just to leave, but to influence anyone. Powerless and prisoners as long as he lived. He had the power to do it. He could stop the children, send them back and make sure the Gods wouldn't be able to bring anyone else. Once he was dead, they would be free again, but with him out of the way, they wouldn't have any targets.

Could he be certain of that? Could he be certain they wouldn't attempt to harm Kiriel, Sivreth or Amerla? Or their descendants? What if they came across someone else who was powerful and decided they were a threat? Pelthiel couldn't be certain that they wouldn't try something like that.

He was ready to let go of the enmity that had brought them to him and Leithia. If he was not who he was, perhaps he would have been left alone, but could he be certain of that? What if they would have come anyway, no matter who he was, only because he was as powerful as he was?

Pel pursed his lips, ignoring the wave of hostility and anger that was pulsing from the Gods. They couldn't harm him, or they would have pushed him off the cliff a long time ago. Not that it would have killed him. But they hadn't even attempted anything. Except this.

He turned to look at them, looking at the anger on their faces, the joy, the confidence. No, he couldn't trust them, not even if he was dead. They were too capricious, too jealous, too full of hatred and anger. They were never going to change and humans were never going to be safe from them. His eyes went back to the ocean. Serityl would be glad to have them. After all, they were the reason she was alone now. Yet, despite all her powers, she might not be able to hold them all. Not together. Not when they would fight her every moment.

He breathed slowly, drawing in each breath with excruciating slowness and letting it out the same way. There was a way for him to bind them and their powers for good. He could do what Zeityl had done, sacrifice himself and bind them with the power of that sacrifice. Serityl wouldn't take him, though, but the army just beyond the wall of water would be more than happy to oblige.

Pel wasn't afraid to die. He hadn't been, not since he had lost Leithia, not since he had learned that the man he had loved was a God and that he had betrayed him. Zeityl might not have killed Leithia, but he didn't save her, either.

And yet... Pel turned to the Gods.

"You're blind and stupid and evil," he said quietly. "Enjoy your victory while it lasts."

He turned and jumped from the cliff, using a spell to float him down to the beach below. It wouldn't be long before the armies reached the shore. Only this time, there wouldn't be a repeat of Nagir. Pel was not young and angry anymore. He was grieving, and he was weary. The pain of Zeityl's betrayal was not worse than the pain of losing him. Pel had been young and angry and Zeityl had never known what it meant to love, either.

*We were bound to break each other. It was always doomed.*

But now, finally, he could rest. And so could Zeityl.

The wall of water wobbled before crashing down. Pel saw the boats sinking and getting smashed to pieces, but he did not move. They would be safe enough. The boats were closer now, and Pel could see eagerness and excitement on the faces of the children who were in them. He could also feel the joyous anticipation of the beings behind him.

The archers in the boats stood steady and took aim. Pel braced himself. The arrows flew towards him, and he closed his eyes.

*Let it bind them.*

"No!" a voice spoke, and it reverberated inside him, across the beach, went through the cliff and the sky, permeated the ocean and the entire universe.

Pel opened his eyes. In front of him stood four familiar figures, but his eyes were drawn to only one. Heldith's eyes were glowing and Pel saw that the entire world was standing still: the arrows, the waves, the breeze, the armies, even the three people with Heldith.

Heldith looked at him, and Pel saw the yearning in his eyes.

"I remember," he said.

# FORTY EIGHT

The look on the Gods' faces might have been comical in different circumstances, but Heldith didn't feel like laughing. There was nothing remotely funny about what had almost happened.

"Zeityl!" Aristyl's voice held such longing, but Heldith hardened his heart as he looked at them.

"What the fuck were you trying to do?" he asked.

"We were trying to avenge you!" Hamithia snapped. "Why are you angry with us?"

"I don't need you to avenge me!" He was furious. "What I did was my choice." His eyes shifted to Pel, who looked pale, but calm. "I will always choose him."

"Over us?" Utfer asked.

"Over anyone or anything,"

Pel's face paled further. "That's a dangerous devotion," he said.

Heldith shrugged. "I have only ever sacrificed myself," he said, understanding what Pel meant even if he didn't say it.

"I wish you hadn't," Pel said, and Heldith's breath caught.

"I never lost you, did I?" he whispered.

"I was nineteen," Pelthiel said. "Your betrayal made me lose my sister... my anger caused me to slaughter thousands... how did you expect me to react?"

Heldith understood. He was twenty now, and if he had been through what Pel had, and learned it had all started with someone he loved and trusted... Heldith understood because he was human, though his soul had grown from Zeityl's, and he held the God's memories. Zeityl had never been human, had never known the kind of love he and Pelthiel had shared, had never been in love and had never had his heart broken. It was no wonder he had thought it had been the end.

"I still shouldn't have done it," he said, realising finally the hurt he must have inflicted on Pel when he sacrificed himself instead of trying to make things right with Pel.

"You came back," Pelt said, as if it was that simple, and perhaps it was.

Heldith looked at the Gods. "I understand why you felt the need to do what you did," he said. "But you are in the wrong. We wronged him. We killed his sister, forced the warriors of Nagir to turn on him when neither he nor his sister had ever done us harm."

"He is their spawn, and would always be a threat!" Ementiar said. "We saw what he did to Nagir."

"Is it worse than what we did to his family?" Heldith asked. "You are ready to burn the world down to avenge me, and you blame him for destroying the city that took his sister from him?"

Amythia opened her mouth as if to argue and Heldith lifted a hand. "Enough," he said. "You won't understand... you can't." He sighed. He loved them, but he couldn't allow them to do this again. "I bind you here," he said. "Till you learn

ompassion and mercy. I bind your powers till you learn how to
top being afraid."

They looked devastated, but angry as well.

*This is what I should have done the last time instead of
roing and throwing myself into the ocean.*

"Please don't do this," Pitoryl said. "We can't stay in this
lace... it... it feels too much..."

"I know," Heldith said quietly. The island held memories
nd emotions, Pelthiel's, Sivreth's, Amerla's, Kiriel's and his own.
That is why you have to stay here."

It was their only chance. He looked at them once more.
He would never stop loving them, no matter what they did, but
e had to do this.

"You're leaving us," Keithia said, sounding bewildered.

"A part of me is Serityl's prisoner," he said. "So, you see,
'm never far from you here. Goodbye for now."

He turned to Pel. "You're coming home with me," he said.
After that, if you wish to leave, I won't stop you, Pel, but you're
ot staying here with them again."

"What do you plan to do about them?" Pel asked, waving
owards the approaching boats.

Heldith looked at them, feeling the same anguish Pel must
ave felt every time the Gods sent someone to fight him.

"Fight and defeat them," he whispered. "And send them
n their way back to their lives."

They might not listen, but he had a feeling he could make
hem.

Pel's lips curved in a smile. "I don't need your help for
hat."

"And yet, you would have sacrificed yourself."

"It seemed the only way." Pel gestured towards his friends.
Why are they here?"

"You can defeat them," Heldith waved to the armies. "Bu only we can convince them. That is why they're here." He smiled at Pel. "Can you trust me and stay out of this?"

Pel looked at him, head cocked to a side, a contemplative look on his face. Heldith was aware of his heart hammering. His skin was clammy and something was squeezing his heart tightly within his chest.

"I trust you in this," Pel said.

Heldith felt his eyes burn and Pel took a step closer, his hands cupping his face, his fingers brushing away the tears.

"I trust you," he said again, and there was a sort of wonder in it, and it was reflected in his eyes too.

Heldith swallowed around the lump in his throat. "Thank you."

It was more than he could have hoped for, but he wouldn't ruin this chance. He wouldn't betray Pel's trust again. Pel smiled and nodded at him as he stepped away and Heldith turned to the ocean and his friends. It was time to end this and to bring Pel home.

Time started again.

# EPILOGUE

P el couldn't sleep. It had been such a long time since he had been out of his island, and in a building full of strangers. Despite the fact that Heldith, Sivreth, Amerla and Kiriel occupied rooms near to his, he still didn't feel comfortable. He rose and tiptoed to the door, opening it silently before stepping outside. The inn was near to the ocean, and he wanted to talk to someone.

Heldith and the others had convinced the youngsters of Pel's innocence, and of the Gods' manipulation, aided with a spell that revealed their memories. The Gods were back on the island, unable to leave while Pel had been able to leave.

Pel left the inn, and walked to the ocean, stopping at its edge, waves lapping his feet, almost caressing them. Serityl seemed to be happy.

"Are you there?" he asked, his voice quiet, his heart aching.

A figure appeared in front of him, above the waves. A person who was as familiar to him as himself, someone that he had never stopped remembering or dreaming about. The one he had wanted to talk to this night.

"Zeityl," he said. "You're here."

"I can't stay for long," Zeityl said softly. "Even though Serityl let me go, there is little left of me after I gave Heldith my powers. Pelthiel... you and I... perhaps we were never meant to be."

"I'm sorry," Pel said. "I'm sorry that I..." What could he say? What was there to even say now?

"Heldith's feelings are his own," Zeityl said quietly. "His soul came from me, but it is not wholly mine. I don't know how you feel about him, but if you care, there is no need for you to hold back."

"It's not that simple," Pel said.

Zeityl smiled. "When has it ever been? But in the end, it is simple, Pelthiel. But it is your choice and your heart. All I want is for you to be happy."

Such a simple thing on the face of it, but was it ever? Pel breathed out, and said, "I'll try. Thank you for everything."

"After everything I caused, this is the least I can do. Pelthiel... I never regretted sacrificing myself for you. All I ever wanted was for you to have a good life, a happy life."

"I wanted to stay away from the world because I was guilty," Pel said. "I wanted to stay away because I was afraid. But I think that perhaps I have paid my penance as well."

He didn't fully believe it, but perhaps he could make up for his previous actions by doing something good now.

"Oh, Pelthiel," Zeityl murmured. "Your heart is still so pure. You don't have to pay any penance."

"That is between me and my conscience," Pel said quietly. "Perhaps I chose the wrong form of penance. Thanks to you, I have the chance now, to do it correctly."

"I won't dissuade you," Zeityl said. "The bit of soul that I
have left will dissipate, and free Serityl. It will not be reborn, but
he will be. Perhaps someday, you and she can be family again. Be
happy, Pelthiel."

The figure disappeared, and all that was left were the
waves lapping at his feet, and the echo of Zeityl's words in his
ears.

"I will try, Zeityl," Pel whispered. "I will try to live well,
do good, and be happy."

It seemed to him that there was a joyous laugh in the
sound of the waves.

*I fill find you, Serityl, once you are reborn.*

*Little one, even if you don't, don't waste your life
searching. You and I will always be family, even if we never find
each other again.*

Pel closed his eyes and felt tears trickle down his cheeks.

"Thank you both," he murmured.

A wave kissed his feet, and went back to the ocean and Pel
smiled, opening his eyes. A sense of peace washed over him. Hope
burgeoned inside, brightening everything.

If you enjoyed this book, please leave a review on the retailer ite from which you purchased this. A review in Goodreads in ddition would make my day.

You may also enjoy my upcoming new release, Curse of ouls, an excerpt from which follows.

## FROM THE CURSE OF SOULS

### ONE

Philip woke up with the remnants of a dream still clinging to him. It was still dark. He couldn't remember what he had dreamt of, but he was overed in sweat and his heart was racing. Casey was next to him, till naked and asleep, cuddled close to him, an arm slung around im. Philip extricated himself slowly, his throat too dry. He vould drink some water and ask the medidroid to look at him ater. If he was coming down with something, he didn't want Casey to get it. Nor did he want to wake his partner at—he lanced at the clock panel display by the bed—3 AM. Besides, he ad a meeting at 9. The second round of meetings with Raylan. Ie had to be in top shape for that.

He went into the bathroom, the lights turning on by hemselves. He took a disposable cup and filled some water, but efore he could drink, he was overcome with a fit of coughing. The cup fell from his hands on to the floor, splashing water all ver. He cursed in between coughs and took a step back.

He found himself drowning; he was in a river, and there vere flat stones which shone on the riverbed. A hand caught his, nd pulled him up, but before he could see the face of his rescuer,

he was back in his bathroom, staring at himself in the mirror, bu
he could feel the burning in his lungs as if he had truly been
drowning. Another fit of the coughs racked him.

What the fuck was happening to him?

Philip straightened, glad for the soundproofing of the
bathroom. At least he didn't wake Casey. He stared at himself in
the mirror, his too pale face and the light brown hair plastered o
his face. Dark, wide eyes stared back at him, fear in their depths.
Sweat had beaded on his face and Philip washed his face and
filled another cup of water and drank it, chasing away the
mingled taste of earth and river water.

"Medical scan," he said, and a medidroid appeared. Philip
waited while the beam of light it directed travelled over his body

"No health issues detected," the droid said in an
emotionless voice. "However, the body shows signs of activation
of Vanarpin curse."

For one moment, Philip couldn't think or move. How wa
it even possible? He forced himself to swallow the panic bubbling
inside him and think. He wished it was Casey, but knew it wasn't
It couldn't be. They had been together for thirteen years now. If i
was Casey, this wouldn't have taken this long. He swallowed and
filled another cup with water, drinking it, trying to chase away
the taste of bile. The water on the floor had pooled around his
feet, and the cold seemed to be seeping into his very marrow.

*I don't want this.*

Vanarpin was not something very common in their world
It had been around for centuries, but considering how rare the
soulmate bond was, it manifested very rarely. Philip tried to
recall the vision of drowning. It had been the Nolaine. He was
certain of it. Those glowing stones on the bed had magic, though
Philip didn't know of what kind.

How ironic that magic had chosen a magical rock to fuck

up Philip's life!

The magic had felt warm and familiar, as did the hand that had found his. Philip had no doubt it had belonged to his soulmate. Bile rose to his throat again. He might hate it, but he needed to remember all the details if he was to get any clues as to who it could be. He knew enough about the disease to know that the vision was often the most important pointer.

He left the bathroom, feeling worse than ever. Casey was snuggled into the blankets, part of his shoulder visible, and an arm, dark against the white sheets. He felt his chest tighten. How was he going to explain this to him? Philip loved Casey. This unknown soulmate was nothing to him. Yet, if he didn't find his soulmate and consummated the bond, the curse would kill him.

Philip wanted to scream. It was so unfair! He swallowed the scream building in his throat and slid back under the covers without waking Casey. It helped that his partner was a heavy sleeper. Philip lay on his back, looking up at the ceiling. He had never looked into Vanarpin, believing he would never get it. In most cases, the bond activated when people were in their early twenties, not late thirties. He thought of the ring in his safe. He had been planning to propose for a while now.

And now this.

In his position, if it became known, Philip might have to let Casey go. Being with another when magic had chosen a soulmate for you was considered downright blasphemous by almost everyone in the world. The bond could not have chosen a worse time to activate. He was in the middle of a war, the only peace in his life within these four walls, with the man at his side. He either had to hide this or let Casey go. If he hid it and someone found out, however, Philip would lose every last bit of credibility he had in the eyes of the men who followed him.

He could feel bitterness coating his mouth. Thirteen years

of togetherness was going to mean nothing to anyone except to him and Casey.

*How can I let him go?*

His own death meant little to Philip. They had been fighting this war for more than fifteen years, and the chances that he wouldn't come out alive at the other end had always been high. None of them knew what the next day was going to bring. Was it the day a drone would level the building they were in? Was this the day a spell would disintegrate the entire city block? There was no saying. That had become so much a part of their lives that it mattered nothing now.

Death might even be easier. It was certainly more familiar. How many people had he lost over the years? He was used to loss, to pain. They all were. Philip's death would not make any difference in the grand scheme of things. His life did, however, and that was what made this so difficult. Philip wasn't foolish enough to think the country would fall apart without him. Yet, he was in the middle of a fucking war that he had not sought, and he couldn't just drop all his responsibilities and die.

All because he loved Casey and didn't want to find his fucking soulmate, who had come thirteen years too late into his life.

Would it have made any difference if they had made an appearance before he had met Casey? Philip didn't know. He didn't want to think or debate. Finding them was not going to be easy, not with the war going on, not when they could be anywhere in the world. Philip wasn't exactly certain how the vision of the stones was going to help. Unless one suddenly appeared in his room with a tracking spell on the thing. He wouldn't put it past magic.

He placed a hand over his chest. It felt no different. Even his breathing was normal now. Was the magic working its way nside, rotting his insides, causing each organ to fail? The damage wasn't irreversible. Not till it got to the point where even the healing magic inherent in him couldn't reverse the effects of Vanarpin. It might be a curse, but it was not so simple. It was both a blessing and a curse. A blessing because it meant magic had chosen someone who was your perfect match. A curse because it was going to kill you if you didn't find them and consummate the bond.

Stone and water. He huffed in annoyance. Why did the Nolaine have an emotional value to his soulmate? Why did those tones have value? Why couldn't he have a soulmate who liked flying, for instance? Who liked being up in the air. Flying was good.

*I would probably be having visions of feathers in that case.*

With his luck, that seemed likely. It was probably what his soulmate had seen. He wasn't sure which would have been easier. Either way, it wasn't going to be possible to keep it a secret. As it was, this was going to come out sooner or later. Right now, it was better for him to be open about this.

Control the narrative.

Philip ignored the way his eyes prickled and throat tightened. His heart felt raw, as if someone had carved up his chest and left it bare. He would get through this. Philip had suffered losses before. He would survive this too.

Philip had to. At least till he got Raylan to sign the peace agreement. Once that had happened, well, then he would be free to live his own life.

Or die, if he so chose.

# ABOUT THE AUTHOR

An author and editor, Niranjan's biggest ambition is to have a character named Garth in every book they write. Niranjan writes books rooted in mythical worlds, and their stories are often a combination of magic and futuristic technology.

When they are not writing or editing, Niranjan can be found cooking or just lying on their couch watching or rewatching C Dramas and writing fanfiction.

More about them may be found at https://authorniranjan.in/

# ALSO BY NIRANJAN

## SERIES

BLUE
BLUE
OUT OF THE BLUE

THE ELITE AND THE ROGUES
THE ELITIST SUPREMACY (BOOK ONE)
RISE OF THE RESISTANCE (BOOK TWO)
FRACTURED ALLIANCES (BOOK THREE)
LINGERING DISCORD (BOOK FOUR)
THE FINAL CONFLICT (BOOK FIVE)
DEEPER CHAOS (FREE BOOK)
THE ELITE AND THE ROGUES (OMNIBUS EDITION)

STANDALONES

SPACES OF SILENCE

THE DEATHLESS ONES

THERE'S ALWAYS A MORNING

WHISPERS IN THE DARK

LIFE REMAINS

BLEEDING GOLD

MAGICAL MAYHEM

THE BANISHED SECRET

THE MANSION

COLLIDING FORCES

THE SOUL OF MAGIC

CHANGES IN THE WIND

THE FLAME OF THE DRAGON'S OATH

GELID ISLANDS (FREE BOOK)

THE DRAGON AND THE MAGE (FREE BOOK)

THE EXILE AND OTHER STORIES (FREE BOOK)*

*AVAILABLE FOR NEWSLETTER SUBSCRIBERS

# Now available for pre-order

## Curse of Souls (19th Jan 2024)

Philip and his partner Casey have been spearheading the secessionist movement in the country of Gedrion, which had escalated into a war with Darren, the tyrant who had been exploiting their people. In a desperate attempt for peace after years of conflict, they approach Raylan, Darren's second-in-command, for an end to the hostilities and to overthrow Darren.

Raylan is as tired of the civil war as his enemies, and he knows that Darren is not one to listen to reason. He has to keep it a secret from everyone on his side that he's meeting with Philip and Casey if he's to give peace a chance.

The last thing any of them expect is for a soul mate bond to spring to life between Philip and Raylan, activating an ancient magic that will kill them both if the bond isn't consummated. With the fate of two nations on the balance, and Philip and Casey's relationship struggling for air, all three men find that they have to make choices none of them are prepared for if they want an end to the war and bring about peace while keeping Philip and Raylan alive.

## Wizard's debt (4th Mar 2024)

When saddled with the guardianship of Ellis, Jeff is prepared for his life to change. It can't get much worse after all. He is a wizard, despised like all of his kind. Life had already caused him to seclude himself away from humanity for centuries with only Derek, his shifter boyfriend, for company. Even with the help, Derek is no better at taking care of children than he is.

*Add in Paris, Ellis' aunt, who wants his custody to herself,
change is going to be rough. Topped off with the mystery behind
the death of Ellis' parents, and the dangerous assailants who have
been stalking and attempting to kidnap Ellis, Jeff finds nothing in
his life is what he has expected.*

*With this relentless mystery group making child rearing
harder than it already was, Jeff and Derek must find a way to
keep them all safe—or die trying. Death might just be their end as
a secret about the murder of Ellis' parents are revealed. Jeff has
grossly underestimated his enemies, and it may be already too
late.*